westland ltd

THE EXORCISM OF SATHISH KUMAR, MBA

Ramiah Ariya is a freelance computer architect by profession. His first short story in Tamil won the second prize from *Kalki* magazine, in 1995. Since then, he has been published in Tamil, both print and online.

The Exorcism of Sathish Kumar, MBA is his first English novel. He blogs at ramsrants.blogspot.com.

The Exorcism of Sathish Kumar, MBA

Ramiah Ariya

Westland Ltd

westland ltd
61, Silverline Building, Alapakkam Main Road, Maduravoyal, Chennai 600 095
No. 38/10 (New No.5), Raghava Nagar, New Timber Yard Layout, Bangalore 560 026
93, 1st Floor, Sham Lal Road, Daryaganj, New Delhi 110 002

First published in India by westland ltd, 2014

10 9 8 7 6 5 4 3 2 1

ISBN: 978 93 84030 19 3

Typeset in Requiem Regular by SÜRYA, New Delhi

To
Sobhana, Prasanna and Vamsi

CONTENTS

PROLOGUE

The hut in the crematorium did not smell of burnt flesh. It had a refreshing odour, and in the time before dawn, with the wind howling outside, I drank deeply of it.

'It's goat's blood,' explained the sorcerer sitting in front of me.

I sat cross-legged and stared at the small fire burning in front of me. The sorcerer could see the entrance to the hut and would warn me if someone came in to attack us. They could, of course, burn down the entire hut, but the sorcerer felt sure they wouldn't. The sick bastards would want videos of us burning.

The 'sick bastards' were from PH Capital, the multinational financial firm. I had not even heard about them till the previous day, but apparently they were very well known in sorcerer circles.

The truth is, yesterday I was a software engineer, not a demon fighter. Any plans I had involved spending the weekend in a bar.

It was four in the morning now, and the sorcerer shook his head. He seemed to be listening carefully. Not to anything earthly.

'You can start,' he said to me finally.

I looked over at the possessed man.

'Are you sure?'

'Yes. Now it's your turn.'

I looked at him sceptically.

'I will take care of your body,' he assured me.

PART I

THE BLAZE WORM

Although my spirit may wander the four corners of the earth,
Let it come back to me again so that I may live and journey here.
Although my spirit may go far away to the flashing beams of light,
Let it come back to me again so that I may live and journey here.
Although my spirit may wander in the valley of death,
Let it come back to me again so that I may live and journey here.

–Rig Veda

I

THE LAYOFF

When I entered the offices of BSD Technologies on the morning of Friday, the thirteenth of November, I was fully expecting to be laid off. In fact, I was hoping they would turn me away at the door. They still had metal detectors at the entrance, as if any self-respecting terrorist would try to bomb us.

No such luck.

A bunch of us got into the lift together and carefully avoided eye contact. I went straight to the cafeteria.

There was not much work. The company had been struggling for the last one month. Now, it was in a freefall. The CEO and founder, Sathish Kumar, had disappeared. His last appearance in public went viral on YouTube. In that video, you can see our beloved leader snarling, shouting and showing his middle finger to Bill Gates at a NASSCOM conference. Then you will see Sathish attempting to storm the stage while shouting obscenities at the titans of Indian industry.

While the whole world was laughing at our company, the layoffs had started quietly.

I had been sure they would have my name near the top of the layoff list. In the last review, I'd been informed that

I was not a Team Player. My manager had talked about the Team as if it were a single organism. I learnt that the Team wanted more work. I abhorred work. It was obvious that the Team hated me. I was bringing them down, according to my manager.

'How can we change this for the better?' he asked.

I thought for a while and then suggested that I could be proactive and create 'win-win' situations.

He did not seem convinced.

But, for some reason, I was not laid off in the first round. There must have been other sundry malcontents in the company. For two weeks, I had watched from my corner as the HR lackeys came and escorted other programmers out. HR people love a layoff. It gives meaning to their existence.

BSD had 2,500 employees, or 'associates' as they call us, in September. Now they had 1,000. The corporate spokesman and public relations officer, Jiten Sharma, claimed that the people laid off were all bad performers. He explained that the top management had an epiphany, one fine morning. They did not want to support bad performers. They were tired and sick of feeding these parasites. From now on, performance was critical for success in BSD. 'You need not apply if you are a parasite,' he thundered to the press.

Nobody was applying for a job at BSD though. Everyone had seen the video of our psycho CEO.

❧

I sat in a corner of the cafeteria by myself. There were a few couples sitting and romancing even though our world was falling apart. The Accounts people were all there in a tight group.

Two of my team members, Raj and Mari, came in. The taller one, Raj, came up to me and whispered, 'I have the List.'

I stared at him.

The quest for the List had finally ended.

A couple of years ago, in a weak, drunken moment, one of my former bosses had told me about the List, and the Keepers of the List.

He said that every corporation has a spreadsheet that is known to very few. It is called the List and it has the names of all the company's employees on it. But the List is not an employee database. It is a layoff list. Employees are split into three categories: the top ten per cent, middle seventy per cent, and bottom twenty per cent.

The bottom twenty per cent are gone if Warren Buffet sneezes and the stock market falls. They get no respect, and are maintained in the company rolls to fill up auditoriums.

The middle seventy are gone if something like the 9/11 attack happens. They get no respect either, but they are tolerated.

The theory is that you can run a company with just ten per cent of its employees. Somehow, the entire top management always finds themselves in the top ten per cent. It's a mystery.

When my former boss told me about the List, I was troubled.

'Am I in the top ten?' I asked him. I was naïve then, much younger.

He laughed hysterically.

The List is like the American drone program. Everyone denies its existence. But people get smoked constantly based on it.

We had been looking for the List for the past two months, just to find out when we could expect HR's kindly touch. And now Raj had found its location.

❧

Mari joined us.

'How did you do it?' I asked Raj.

'It was difficult,' he said.

'But how? This must be the first time in history that a non-Keeper has found the List . . .'

Raj coughed. 'I am not just a non-Keeper.'

'You mean . . .'

'Yes, in the bottom twenty, baby . . .' He did not seem bothered by it.

I was worried.

'Where am I?'

He became serious.

'I don't know.'

'My name is not on the List?'

'It is, but it's weird. You have to come and see it.'

On the way down I asked Raj again how he had found the List.

'Well, I asked myself how they would keep the List current, you know? They've laid off so many people. If they don't keep the List up-to-date, they will end up laying off the same person again and again.'

Mari thought that would keep HR busy.

'Yes, so they must be linking this to the employee database in some way. I have access to that database and ended up snooping a little bit. There was this mysterious feed going somewhere, and it ended up being the List.'

We walked over to his computer.

'Take a look.'

The List was colour coded. There was green, which I assumed meant top ten. There were a lot of names with yellow. A few with red.

'Where is my name?' I asked Raj.

He scrolled to the top of the list – it was the first one. My name was on top of the List. The spreadsheet cell said 'Arjun Palani' in bold, and in purple. The next column had a date – 13 November 2012.

I stared at it for some time.

Why?

'There is a comment on the cell,' Mari said.

Raj hovered the mouse over the cell. A tiny yellow box opened up. It said, 'Marked for the EXM team; Do NOT remove'.

∾

I was spooked. The company's List had me marked for some reason. Could it be that I was actually considered . . . smart? So smart that they had me identified among a thousand for a special team?

The possibility that I was smart had occurred to me earlier in my career, but I had dismissed it repeatedly. Particularly after being laid off three different times.

Perhaps they saw potential in me – a spark of greatness.

'Perhaps the EXM team collects garbage,' Mari said.

Envious bastard.

'Whatever it is, you'll know soon,' Raj said. 'That's today's date.'

'I'm prepared for whatever my company offers me,' I said with conviction. I had newfound respect for BSD's managers.

Just then, our manager walked past, glaring at us. Early during the layoffs, he had seen us loitering around. Immediately he had exercised his leadership ability and commanded us to work. We pointed out that there was no work. He had then cursed us for showing no initiative. He had nothing to threaten us with and watched us wander around with impunity.

'Sir . . .' Raj called him.

Our manager stopped, but kept looking away like a Seventies villain.

'Sir, when is the EXM team starting work?'

He finally turned fully to us and said, 'What team?'

'The EXM team. Is it a new client, Sir?'

'I've never heard of any such team,' he said and walked away.

'Is there a Teams list?' I asked.

Raj went back to his computer to look.

'Hey, aren't you both in the bottom twenty? Aren't you worried, you lazy bums?' I asked.

'The List is not read-only,' Mari shrugged.

'You mean you upgraded yourself?'

'As we deserve, for finding the List in the first place.'

'There is no EXM team listed,' Raj said from his terminal.

We pondered this for some time.

'Where did you look?' asked Mari.

'In the employee database.'

'Do you have access to Accounts?'

'Not to the really important stuff, but I have access to some spending records.'

Raj started typing again.

At that moment, the lift door opened and two security guards stepped out. The HR director, Dileepan, came out with them. They looked in our direction. The HR director said something to the guards, and all three started walking towards us.

We froze. Raj was still on the Accounts database. I wanted to warn him, but could not say anything. Was this the moment that we would all be arrested for cybercrime? Was I getting laid off a freaking fourth time? Why the security guards?

Dileepan walked up the long corridor with the guards on either side; he looked like Al Pacino in some gangster movie. Heads craned from cubicles. The guards' heels clicked rhythmically on the tiles.

Raj was still typing.

As they came closer, Dileepan inclined his head and the guards stopped. He smiled at me. I have no doubt he understood the effect his show was having on everyone.

'Arjun Palani?'

'Yes Sir.'

'I am Dileepan.'

'Yes Sir.'

'Could you collect your bag and any belongings and come with me?'

I gave Mari a despairing look. Raj was peeking out from behind his computer.

I silently went to my desk and picked up my bag. It felt very heavy. The whole floor was now watching me: the guy who had messed up so much, his dismissal was being handled by the great HR director himself.

The guards turned around smartly and I started walking with them. Dileepan patted me on my back as I walked past him. Tears stung my eyes.

2

THE EXM TEAM

When we got into the lift, I assumed we would go to the HR department, but we got off on the seventh floor. The guards stepped out first, looked around, and then waved us out.

The floor looked like a garbage dump. Chairs were overturned, broken. Cubicle walls had collapsed. There were holes in the walls.

I stared at the holes while marching up a corridor. It was as if they were sprayed on the wall; and at one point there were red smears. They looked like bullet holes I had seen in movies.

'Don't worry about those. They are from the second assault last week,' Dileepan said, following me.

We kept walking. What was the second assault? What was the *first*?

There was a steel door in front of us. It looked like a vault. I turned to look at the corridor behind me. My eyes caught a flash of brightness.

There was a gun barrel staring at us from a hole in the wall.

'Keep walking,' Dileepan said.

Finally we reached the steel door. It had a small console

on the right. Dileepan peered at it, trying to locate something. I glanced back. I could still see a couple of gun barrels, now turned towards the door.

My phone vibrated.

'Sir,' I said.

'Hold on.'

He must have been keying in some password, because the steel door now started opening inward.

'There are guns here,' I said.

'Ignore them. They won't shoot us,' he said. After a pause, he added, 'Although, it wouldn't hurt to keep your hands where they can see them.'

There was a flight of stairs in front of us and we started climbing them.

I gathered some courage and asked, 'Are you going to fire me, Sir?'

Dileepan laughed aloud. It echoed in the small cavern.

He did not answer.

∾

We finally reached the eighth floor. Dileepan opened a door and ushered me in.

Three people were sitting at a rectangular table. They turned around abruptly when I came in. In fact, it seemed like they were about to duck under the table. Dileepan followed me in and closed the door.

The room was big and had wires all over it. There was a projection screen in front of us, displaying a strange portrait – an image of a man sitting atop a buffalo. It looked like the god of death, Yama.

The man sitting closest to the screen said, 'You must be Arjun.'

Dileepan clapped his hand on my shoulder and said, 'The man himself.'

I was confused. All the executive managers were there. The man who had spoken to me was the chief operating officer of BSD – his name was Madhan. Next to him was Keerthi, a woman I recognized as the vice-president of HR. On the opposite side sat the CFO, Aman, who was now running the company.

This did not seem like a mere firing session. Perhaps they were tapping me for the new CEO?

In olden days, in India, there was a practice of choosing a king by the elephant-garland method. They handed a garland to the previous king's elephant and asked it to go find the next king. The elephant usually wandered around and chose some beggar guy sleeping on the road. Although there were cases of the elephant handing over the garland and then trampling the recipient, it seemed a good, effective way to choose a king. I've always thought modern CEOs should be chosen the same way. Give an elephant a garland and have him walk around corporate corridors.

Maybe they found me through some similar lottery system.

Aman, the CFO, pointed to a corner and said, 'Sit down and do not speak unless spoken to.'

Hey, that is no way to talk to your new boss.

I sat down meekly. Dileepan leaned against the door and winked at me. I had an uncomfortable feeling that he was making sure I did not run out.

They all turned their attention back to the screen. Aman tapped a key on his computer keyboard and the screen changed to a project plan. They stared at it.

I put my hand in my pocket and pulled out my phone

surreptitiously. There was a new message from Raj. I opened it.

Do NOT join the EXM team!!!!

❧

'Arjun!' called someone.

I looked up from my phone.

The VP HR, had turned around and she was smiling at me. Everyone in the room was looking at me.

'How are you?'

'I'm fine, Madam.'

She smiled again.

'We have heard so much about you.'

Really?

'Whenever I talk to your manager, what's-his-name, he is singing your praises.'

I became suspicious. That was highly unlikely.

The people in the room were all looking at me, smiling and nodding as Keerthi spoke. It was creepy.

She looked at me expectantly. I had nothing to say.

'Okay, Arjun, how would you like to take your career to the next level?'

They were all still nodding.

'Yes? How would you like to really . . .' she was looking for words '. . . really challenge your capabilities?'

I did not want to do that. I did not have much in terms of capabilities.

'How would you like to take this company to the next level? Hmmm? Explore new horizons? Go beyond your wildest imagination?'

She stopped. There was an uncomfortable silence.

'Okay, Madam,' I said with zero enthusiasm.

'Good,' she said. She looked at a paper in her hand. 'You are not married, are you?'

'No, Madam.'

'Any close relatives?'

'No, Madam.'

She turned and looked at Aman. He gave her the thumbs-up sign.

'Can you sign this document?' she said, turning back to me.

I took the sheaf of papers she handed over.

The first page said: 'EXM – Release Contract'.

'Keerthi, can you just ask him to sign it?' Aman said tersely.

I looked up and tried to say something. Keerthi gave me a winning smile.

'Just sign it. It is a standard release contract.'

'Do I have a choice? Don't I have to read it?' I asked, mustering up courage.

They all looked at Dileepan. He was still leaning against the door.

'Do you want to be fired a fourth time?' he asked.

No, I did not want that.

'Do you trust us?' asked Keerthi.

Not really.

I picked up my pen and signed the document.

'Welcome to the EXM team,' Keerthi said.

At that moment, a snarling sound and a crash came from behind one of the room's walls. The walls rattled.

I looked around, panicked. Everyone else was still looking at me. They did not seem perturbed.

'Welcome,' repeated Aman.

❧

When I was young, I went to a government school. One day, we were digging pits in the school grounds for no real reason, when I found a bone. It looked like a human ankle bone; all my friends were properly horrified. I took it home with pride and got beaten up by my father.

He told me that day that the bone's owner, the spirit that lived in that body, would follow me home in the night. He promised he would do nothing to protect me. In fact, he would point the spirit to my bed and say, 'There you go, Mr Spirit. That is the nasty boy who digs up bones.'

That night was one of the most terrifying I've had in my life. I spent the whole night listening to every creak, every creepy whisper of wind, and imagining that the spirit was coming to bite my leg off in revenge. I resisted going to the bathroom and was wide awake most of the night. Finally, hovering between sleep and wakefulness, I had heard a shriek. It was an unearthly sound, surely from the depths of the spirit world. I woke up fully, shaking; discovered that I had wet myself.

I was sure it was a spirit for a long time. Even in college I was reluctant to go out alone in the night. It took an intense period of atheism to cure me of the fear (I was probably the only person in the world who took to atheism to improve my bathroom habits).

That fear was back, now, as I sat in the eighth floor conference room. The snarl sounded familiar.

The screen was now displaying a project plan. It had three tasks.

1. Get ganja
2. Get the girl
3. Get dimethyl tryptamine

They were all assigned to me.

Aman turned to me and said, 'Can you do that? Get ganja?'

'I have heard of Ganja, but I have not worked with that technology . . .' I said.

Madhan and Keerthi laughed at my answer. Aman just said, 'Not technology.'

'Ganja . . . as in the drug?' I asked.

'Yes. What else?'

'You want me to get some ganja for you? That is the task?'

'Yes,' he said impatiently.

'Isn't that illegal?'

Dileepan guffawed.

'That has not bothered you before, right?' Aman asked.

I was indignant. 'What do you mean? I have never had ganja. And what sort of a request is this anyway?'

'It is not a request,' Dileepan said. 'And do not take that tone again.'

'But . . . is this some kind of a joke? How will I get ganja?'

'You should know. Aren't you a drug addict?' said Keerthi.

'Wha . . . No. What do you mean?'

There was silence in the room. Aman looked at Dileepan.

'But you look like a drug addict,' Keerthi said.

I was wounded. Other people had told me this, of course. I assumed they were jealous of my personality. I really had never done drugs; the last thing I wanted was to hallucinate about spirits.

'Thanks. But I am not a drug addict. Now, can I get out of this?' I said.

Dileepan straightened and shifted his massive frame.

'Let us not hear any more talk of getting out, shall we?'

Madhan intervened and said, 'Arjun, you are a part of the team. Let us work together.'

I gestured at the project plan and said, 'All the tasks are assigned to me. That does not seem much like team effort.'

'But, come on. The rest of us need to plan strategy,' he said.

A horrible thought came to me.

'Hold on,' I said. 'You did not choose me just because I look like a drug addict, did you?'

There was an uncomfortable silence.

'Of course not,' said Aman.

'Why exactly did you choose me for this team then?' I asked.

Dileepan muttered impatiently. He looked like he wanted to wring my neck.

'We will explain it to you by tonight,' Aman said smoothly. 'We have a big operation coming up this evening, so please bear with us.'

He swung his chair around to glance at the screen.

'Okay, now back to the task at hand. How can we get some quantity of ganja?' he continued.

They all looked at me again. They really seemed to think I would know the answer.

I had to admit, the request was intriguing. Maybe IT companies had turned a corner. Maybe they'd found out that someone in Apple or Google smoked marijuana, and now wanted to 'innovate' by forcing everyone to smoke pot. It was possible that Gartner Research or Harvard Review had a paper out on the efficiency gains using cocaine. Who knew?

Perhaps if I figured this out, I could stay here. Even if they fired me, I would at least have the ganja.

'What about the police?' I asked.

'I know someone at the commissioner's office,' said Dileepan.

HR guys always know someone at the commissioner's office.

Dileepan brought out a bag and fished around in it. He dropped a heavy gadget on the table.

'Walkie-talkie,' he said.

I picked it up. It had a display screen, a tiny one; and some switches.

'How do I operate it?'

'Read the manual,' he growled, extending his hand.

'What?' I asked.

'Your cell phone.'

'I need it. What if there is an emergency?'

'Keerthi, can you clarify the terms to our man?' Aman said.

'Yes, of course. Arjun, your contract binds you to a non-compete, non-disclosure and a non-solicit. You cannot reveal any of our conversations here to anyone outside. Particularly to the employees or other contractors and mercenaries of PH Capital.'

'Mercenaries?'

'Please hand over your cell phone and make no contact with anyone.'

'It must be easy for you, being a geek,' said Madhan. Somehow that cracked them up; they began laughing hysterically.

Clank, clank, came a sound from an adjoining room.

It was the sound of metal chains. Then I heard heavy

footfalls. Someone was pacing back and forth. Again, they all went silent and looked at me.

'We're running out of time,' Aman said.

Thus it was that, on that sunny day, I found myself outside the gates of BSD, with a walkie-talkie jutting out of my pocket. It was the only proof that I was part of the EXM team.

3
GETTING THE GANJA

I remembered Keerthi's warning about contacting other people. That led me straight into an internet parlour, where I signed into Gmail. I thought of blasting a Facebook status about what I was doing, and then thought the better of it.

Raj was online as I expected.

'I am part of management,' I typed.

'Where are you?' he replied.

I waited.

'You are part of the EXM team?' he asked.

'Yes, technically I am your superior now,' I replied.

'It will not last long.'

'I smell jealousy.'

'I found out more information about them.'

'I'm honour-bound to report you to my teammates.'

He was silent.

'Tell me more, Commoner.'

'Listen, be careful. I found their team mission, vision and so on. It seems they want to exorcise some demon from the CEO.'

'Demon?'

'Yes, probably a metaphor. I assume they mean that they

are going to restructure the organization or something. Without the founder's permission. In fact, I think they have him locked up somewhere. That is what it implies in the vision statement.'

'Dude, what is with these managers and vision statements?'

'I know.'

There was a short gap in the conversation. I was debating whether to tell Raj about the ganja.

'Why are you not calling me?' Raj asked.

'Don't have phone. Dileepan took it from me.'

'WHAT???'

'Don't worry, I think they have better phones.'

'But . . . Arjun! The phone has my messages!!'

'Hmmm . . .'

'Dileepan is going to come after me!!'

I cursed myself. I should have deleted the messages.

'Okay, so here is the thing. These EXM guys have some document protected with a password. I am trying to crack it. I don't need Dileepan on my back now,' Raj typed.

'Why are you trying to crack everything Raj? Why don't you just trust your betters?'

'Shut up . . . you have gone over to the dark side. This document could save your butt.'

'Okay, can you help me with something?'

'What?'

'Where do I get some ganja in Chennai?'

There was no reply.

'Hey, can you let me know now? I'm in a hurry.'

'Arjun, who asked you to get ganja?'

'Our team. It is my first assignment.'

'If I were you, I would go home now. You have no idea what they are pulling you into.'

'Ganja, please.'
'Google ganja and exorcism.'
He went offline.

❧

Maybe I could find ganja in Chennai through Google?
It was an idea.
Maybe even on eBay.
I typed 'ganja' and 'exorcism' in Google and idly scrolled through the results.

It seemed ganja was available during Vedic times. It was mentioned in the Atharvana Veda. I could totally understand why the Vedic priests were stoned most of the time. On the other hand, they were probably talking about Ganga, not ganja – and some white guy translating was having fun at our expense.

There was a passionate discussion on a website about the drink Soma – some thought it was a mushroom and others thought it was ganja. Team Mushroom was getting aggressive and calling Team Ganja names.

Of course, ganja was used for all kinds of medical problems. Some doctors prescribed it for everything from nausea to cancer.

And then, it was also used to calm people possessed by demons. In particular, it stimulated appetite. So these crazy people would become hungry and follow their feeders like lambs.

This seemed like a bad idea to me. I would not want some possessed person to become extremely hungry and start looking for blood. But what do I know?

So exorcists used ganja to control possessed people.
Interesting.

Perhaps whoever was screaming and snarling in the seventh floor was possessed? It seemed more likely that they were drugged and hungry.

I did not really believe in possession. It would also be way too weird for an already weird day.

∾

One of the ganja forums in Chennai said the plant was actually being cultivated in the middle of the city. It also gave the address of a website that had an online chat where you could discuss whatever you wanted.

In other words, there seemed to be a customer service centre for selling ganja. I liked that.

I went to the website and chose to chat with a 'representative'.

''sup?' said the chat window.

Very cool.

'Need some ganja,' I typed.

'How much?'

Hmmm . . . problem. How much did I need?

I opened the walkie-talkie and punched the Connect button. The display in the walkie-talkie said, 'Aman'.

'Hello?'

'Hi, yes Arjun, what do you need?'

It was Aman's voice, crystal clear.

'Ummm . . . how much ganja are we talking about?'

Silence.

The chat window said, 'Man, u there?'

'S, hold on,' I typed.

'U trying 4 first time?'

'S.'

Then it occurred to me that he might hike up the price. So I typed, 'No'.

'It is standard price,' he replied.

Smart guy.

Madhan's voice came in: 'Hey, how about fifty grams?'

Keerthi's voice: 'We tried that the last time. Sathish is too used to that. Remember, he tried to bite my arm off?'

Madhan: 'Oh ya.'

I was shocked. So they did have the CEO Sathish with them. And why was he trying to bite other peoples' arms?

There was silence. Maybe Aman was telling them off for revealing too much.

Aman's voice: 'All right Arjun, get a hundred grams.'

I typed, '100 g' in the chat window.

'Whoa! Is it a corporate party?'

'S.'

'That is a lot. Particularly with the raids.'

I sat up.

'What raids?'

'Police cracking down on ganja in city. They have most of it now.'

I did not want to get involved with the police.

'r u in trouble?' I typed.

'Ha . . . no . . . police can't come in here.'

I wondered where he was based.

'It is going to cost u.'

'How much?'

'An ounce is 5000. 100 grams is 17000.'

I flipped open the walkie-talkie.

'It is going to cost 17000,' I said into it.

Aman: 'Approved.'

There was no other response. I waited for a couple of seconds.

'Hello, guys?'

Madhan: 'Yes, Arjun?'

'I appreciate the approval, but how are you going to pay for it?'

Madhan: 'You can pay; get a receipt and submit an expense statement—'

I cut in.

'Hello, I am not going to pay for it. And I won't get a receipt anyway.'

Silence again.

The chat window said: 'They fighting over who pays for it?'

I typed 'S'.

'Freaking corporates. All the same. Tell them they can pay thru Paypal. Damn idiots.'

∾

I left the internet parlour and got into an auto-rickshaw. The ganja rep had told me to get to Adyar signal and wait there till someone showed up to guide me. We had already paid, so it was probable that I would be waiting at Adyar signal the whole day and not see any ganja.

I slid back in the auto-rickshaw seat and closed my eyes. I had browsed anonymously and showed no ID to the parlour manager. Till now, I could not be held for having done anything illegal. I suspected that the CEO of my company was under the influence of drugs; I had no idea whether he was being kept against his wishes or otherwise. I was not an accessory to anything.

I could just leave at this point and go home.

But, it would not stop there. My managers would come after me, I was sure of that. They hated insubordination, particularly from someone way below their class.

I was doomed when they identified me as an EXM team member, for whatever reason. Anonymity pays in an organization; and I had made some mistake that had brought me to their attention.

To a certain extent, I did look forward to their appreciation if I delivered the ganja package. I had been fired thrice before, for not 'performing' to expectations. My previous managers had told me I was not a team player; not a goal-oriented person; not a person with a positive attitude. I did not have the 'can-do' spirit. Three years out of college, I had learnt that I was pretty dispensable in an organization.

Now, I was ready to go underground to prove otherwise.

It was noon, and Adyar signal was busy. I stood in front of a clothing store as the rep had instructed. Maybe they had the ganja in the store. A couple of people were peering at me from inside.

Someone tapped me on the shoulder. I turned and there was a geek standing in front of me – thick glasses, buttoned-up half-shirt, bag hanging from a shoulder, earnest-looking. He was the epitome of a geek.

'Hi, Kamal?' he asked in a high-pitched voice.

'Yes.' I had played Bond and given a false name.

'Please come with me.'

He had a motorbike. It looked ancient. We got on and raced towards Guindy.

Between Guindy and Adyar in the east lies the Indian Institute of Technology campus. Next to this campus there are a few monuments and then the state governor's palatial mansion, the Raj Bhavan. That whole area, from IIT to the end of Raj Bhavan is the Reserve Forest of Guindy. It is one of the few forests left within the city of Chennai. The forest is also a deer sanctuary.

The IIT campus is a part of the sanctuary.

My escort turned into the campus. We rode on amidst dense trees on either side. The road was smooth, well-laid.

We went past the administrative buildings and academic departments. I could see the famed water tank built by the civil engineering students of yore. It had been empty since day one, because they had failed to take the water's weight into consideration while building it. So, the water tank will collapse if you add water.

We went deeper, into unfamiliar territory. I wondered if he was a college student.

Then he took a sharp turn onto a path that led into the forest. We bumped along a little bit. When we could no longer see the road behind us, the bike stopped.

In front of us was a wall with a small gate built in.

'Please go through,' he said.

I walked through the gate.

The other side was dense forest, but a path led through it. I walked along. After a couple of minutes, I reached a clearing. A concrete room was built in the middle of it.

In front of that room, there was a man, smoking. He was leaning against the building. He beckoned me.

I walked up to him.

Close up, he looked like a professor. Clean shirt, well-pressed pants. Scholarly glasses. French beard. He looked around forty.

'Kamal?' he asked.

'Yes, Sir.'

'Welcome.' He walked into the room and I followed him inside.

Bookshelves lined the walls of the room. A table stood in the centre of the room, and there were books on it too. Two chairs. He asked me to sit.

I looked at the books. One title was *Solving the Schrodinger Equation: Has Everything Been Tried?*

Another was *Topics in General Theory of Relativity and Newtonian Gravitation.*

The guy really was a professor.

'You asked for a big amount,' he said.

'Yes, Sir.'

'I see you have already paid for it. Here's your stuff.'

He pulled out a nice canvas packet and placed it in front of me.

I looked around.

'Aren't you afraid of the police?' I asked.

'They can't come in here. It is an academic campus,' he replied.

So the professor and his students were growing ganja in the forest. I liked this. Thumbing their nose at authority. It probably helped their doctoral dissertations or whatever they did in college.

'I liked physics in college,' I said.

He looked distracted. 'I am sorry,' he said.

'What for?'

The room darkened. I turned towards the door.

The biggest guy I have seen in my life was filling up the door with his frame.

ॐ

The man looked like someone from WWF. He bent down and walked in, placed a photograph on the table. Then he peered at me.

I glanced at the photograph. It was a shot of me leaving the BSD premises in the morning. My face was pretty clear, along with the clothes I was wearing.

'FBI,' he said.

My throat went dry. I glared at the drug dealer/professor.

'You said the police won't come here.'

He shrugged.

'What is your name?' the big guy asked me.

'Kamal.'

'Can you step out with me, please?'

I got up. The FBI might not have jurisdiction here, but I was not going to argue jurisdiction with The Hulk.

We walked out into the mid-day sun and I saw three other white guys standing there. They all wore sunglasses and were impeccably dressed.

'He is our guy,' the big guy growled.

They stared at me for a few seconds. I was uncomfortable: the ganja packet was still in my hand.

'Search him,' the man in the middle said.

The big guy asked me to empty my pockets. A credit card fell out, and so did my driver's licence, with my real name on it. So much for playing the spy. He picked up the walkie-talkie and inspected it.

'Listen, Mr Arjun, you are in deep trouble,' said the guy in the middle, with the licence in his hand.

'Yes, Sir.'

'You work for BSD?'

'Yes.'

'You understand that they are under investigation for offences in the United States?'

This was the first time I was talking to a white guy in my life. I usually had trouble understanding English in Hollywood movies, but this man spoke without an accent.

'I did not know that, Sir.'

They all looked at each other.

'Ah. You are innocent, but you're collecting cannabis for them?'

I did not know what he meant by cannabis, so I just kept nodding. It was a technique that had proved useful in school.

'Yes, Sir.'

They all started laughing. I smiled as well. Oh, these funny Americans.

'Where is your ID?' I said, laughing.

The laughing stopped.

'What was that?'

'Your ID, that shows you're with the FBI?'

The big guy caught me by the scruff of my neck. He then proceeded to squeeze it.

It felt like I was drowning. I started flailing and dropped the ganja package. One of the guys in front of me calmly walked over and picked it up. I struggled with the big guy's vise-like hands, while the three others watched. They were looking straight into my eyes.

Was I going to die?

I could hear a loud noise in my head, and realized it was blood being squeezed in.

Out of the corner of my eye I could see the professor rushing about, waving his hands. He was saying something to the Americans.

Just as I felt like consciousness was slipping, the hands relaxed. I dropped to the floor, heaving and coughing.

They all waited. I did not want to get up. I kept my hands on my head and sat down on the ground.

The guy in the middle walked up to me and kneeled down. He put a finger under my chin and lifted my head.

'Take the package and go over to BSD. If you reveal one word about what happened here, we will do this again – but we won't stop.'

I got up slowly. They thrust the ganja package in my hand. I turned around and stumbled back.

∽

I could feel tears streaming down my face. Being a grown man and getting beaten up is not good for your ego. I wanted to run back and punch the guy who had attacked me, fully knowing that he could break me like a twig.

Damn the FBI! Down with American imperialism!

I reached the gate in the wall and passed through. Then I stopped. I looked at the bag in my hand. It seemed heavier.

I slowly raised it to eye level and peered at it.

I remembered the professor giving me a bag that had some letters printed on one side. This bag had no writing on it.

I realized someone could still be watching me and walked on.

They had switched the bags on me.

It did not make sense. Why give me a different bag of ganja? Is that all they wanted to do? To switch the bags? They could have switched it before I went to the damn place. Maybe they did want to send a message. And wanted me to deliver a different bag. This could be rice flour, for all I knew.

I caught the bike service back to Adyar, and within half an hour was back at the gates of BSD.

4

MEETING MISS MALINI

I had mixed feelings when I walked into the eighth floor conference room. On the one hand it seemed they were under some kind of investigation. They also probably had the CEO in their custody; and had sent me on an illegal mission.

But, for the very first time, I had accomplished a task, done what the managers wanted.

Would they appreciate it? Did I 'meet expectations'? Or was I below par? Perhaps I did not glow with positive energy while performing the task.

They all cheered when I walked in. I even thought I heard a grunt of approval from the next door demon or drug-addict.

'We knew we could trust you,' said Madhan.

Aman gave me a thumbs up. I put the package on the desk. Dileepan opened it.

He took a small quantity between two fingers and sniffed it.

'Good quality,' he said. 'Not like last time.'

'I think we should try it out on him,' Keerthi said.

Aman held up his hand.

'Arjun, I think you should rest before your next

assignment. Dileepan will take you to the lounge.'

I had turned to go, when he said, 'By the way, what is on your neck?'

My neck was still sore from the friendly massage by the Yankee. Perhaps there were some bruises. They all peered at my neck.

'Yes, what happened? You look like you tried to hang yourself and failed,' said Dileepan.

I touched my neck gingerly, unable to think of an explanation. 'Nothing . . . I have to take a look,' I said finally. It was a lame answer.

Aman did not say anything.

'You did not run into Big Bruce, did you?' Madhan asked.

'Who's that?'

'You know you're not supposed to hide anything from us, by contract, right?' Keerthi said.

The contract was sounding more and more like the *Manu Smriti* or some fatwa.

'I think we should make things clearer,' Aman said. 'Sit down, Arjun.'

I sat on the nearest chair.

'Have you heard of PH Capital, the hedge fund managers?'

'No.'

'Okay, I do not have time for a detailed explanation. But they have a bunch of mercenaries here, in Chennai. They are trying to stop us from accomplishing our goals.'

Goals such as drugging the CEO and taking over the company?

'They use unprofessional means of persuasion to make their point. They have encountered Madhan. He was not persuaded, and decided to contribute more towards our vision.'

Wow. So Madhan got squeezed too. I could not resist looking him over to see if there were any physical signs of the persuasion. He did not look too pleased with this revelation.

'If you had an encounter, or even saw a few Caucasian guys following you in the pursuit of one of your assignments, you have to communicate it to us. That information may help us take a) evasive action b) re-evaluate our threat matrix and c) mitigate our risk.'

'Okay, what is a Caucasian?'

'A white dude,' Dileepan said.

I shook my head. 'I didn't see any.'

It was possible they were from the FBI; it was also possible that they were not, and were really from PH Capital. But I was not going to tell on them here, and risk being an accessory. I had heard that the United States government needed very little reason to throw someone into Guantanamo Bay. As far as I was concerned, PH Capital and the FBI could be one and the same.

They looked at each other.

'Okay, you can go and rest,' Aman said.

I left for the lounge.

∾

The lounge was a luxurious big bedroom, with a flat-screen television in a corner. It had an attached bathroom, and a huge window with a view of Old Mahabalipuram Road, or the IT Corridor stretch of Chennai. Far below, traffic was snaking its way on both sides.

On a coffee table, there was lunch ready for me. Dileepan

did not look happy about leaving me there. I thought he was worried about me stealing the silverware.

I went into the bathroom and looked at myself in the mirror. There were quite clearly marks on my neck. They did not look like finger imprints though. It was as if two pythons had wound themselves around my neck.

Cruel bastard.

After lunch I walked over to the window and peered down. This stretch of the IT corridor was not fully done, and there were ditches on both sides. I saw a few cars parked opposite our gates. There was a police van there too.

I thought about the photo that Bruce had shown me, taken when I was leaving these gates this morning. Since they did not know anything about me at that point, they must have someone posted there constantly, photographing everyone. That meant someone in one of those cars parked opposite the gates. Or perhaps in one of the buildings opposite.

They could still be watching the gates for all I knew. And if they were, they would know when I left for my second task.

That was not a good thing. I did not want Big Bruce following me around.

From somewhere in the building I heard a wild scream. It was not very loud and faded away almost instantly.

There was a small commotion below. A couple of policemen walked out of the building. They had a person between them, in handcuffs. Just as they were about to shove him into the van, he looked up.

It was Raj.

Did he get arrested for cracking open some secret

document? I knew he would get in trouble at some point for that.

This was not good. Raj and Mari were my closest friends. We formed a non-team-player team.

Raj got into the van awkwardly, and it took off.

It was possible that Dileepan had got him arrested for prying into the EXM team. Too much of a coincidence otherwise. Perhaps I could talk to Aman and get him released.

There was a knock on my door.

'They want you back,' said Dileepan.

I did not want to leave 'my' room. It was surprising how quickly I had adapted to luxury.

∾

The screen in the conference room now displayed a photograph. It was a girl, probably in college. It had been taken when she was stepping out of a house.

The people around the room all looked worried and harassed.

'Hi,' Aman said distractedly.

Keerthi had her head on the table. She sat up and looked at me with bloodshot eyes. Then she turned away. Her right cheek had what looked like a scratch on it.

'We're running out of time. The ganja seems to have made things worse,' Madhan said.

'He's probably building resistance to it,' Aman said.

'I'm not going in there again,' Keerthi said.

They did not seem to care anymore that I was listening to their 'secret' conversations.

'Dileepan, isn't the ganja good quality?' asked Aman.

'Yes, I am sure it is.'

'Where did you get it from, Arjun?'

'From the IIT campus,' I said truthfully.

'You sure it was not tampered with?'

'I just got the package and came back,' I said, less truthfully.

'I think we should get Malini here, as soon as possible. Otherwise, we will all be killed,' Keerthi said.

'Do not say her name aloud,' Aman said angrily.

The footfalls behind the walls resumed. *Clank, clank* sounded some chains.

'Okay, Arjun, we have to get this girl to come here,' said Aman.

'Who is she?'

'We cannot talk about the details now. I have a dossier with her address. Just go and bring her here.'

'What if she refuses to come?'

'You may have to fool her; or convince her in some other way,' Madhan said.

'What other way? This sounds like kidnapping to me. I am not going to kidnap a girl.'

Aman sighed. 'Listen, Arjun, why don't you just talk to her? By the way, when you meet her, keep the walkie-talkie switch on, so we can listen.'

'That sounds creepy.'

'No, really not. It is for your own good. We may be able to talk to her. She may listen to someone from her . . .' Aman struggled with words for the first time.

'Someone from her class, level?' I said.

He did not say anything.

I shrugged. 'Okay, give me the file on her. I'll go talk to her.'

'You have to memorize what is in this. We have to destroy it,' said Madhan, handing me a green file.

I opened it.

The first page had a large picture of the girl. It was a nice photograph, attractive. I stared at it for some time until someone coughed.

The next page simply had her name, landline phone number, cell phone number and address. She lived in the Mylapore area, a few miles to the north.

The page after that said she had just completed her Bachelor's degree (political science) at some private college. She was looking for work. Political science and work – maybe we could just offer her a job at BSD.

That was it. Just three pages in the file. I memorized her address and phone numbers and handed back the file reluctantly – I wanted to keep the photograph.

'Are you ready?' asked Madhan.

'I am. But I think we may have a problem. I think your enemies could be watching the gate. If I go out, they may follow me,' I said.

'How do you know they're watching us?'

'Just guessing.'

'You could jump over the back fence,' said Keerthi. She was still hiding the right side of her face from me.

'It's too high. And they could be watching there as well. Can't one of you drop me in your car?'

'We cannot leave this room,' said Madhan.

'Yes, none of us can step out of this building anyway. We will be taken out,' said Aman.

They seemed to be serious. What the hell were they caught up in?

'But,' Aman continued, 'we can create a distraction for you.'

He gestured at Dileepan.

'We can lay off a bunch of people, and you can just go out with them. Nobody will notice you.'

Pretty callous. But it could work.

∾

The people laid off seemed happy. They were clustered around the entrance. It had been an express checkout, arranged for my benefit.

A couple of them knew me. They came over and wanted to know how many times I would be laid off in a day.

'We saw you leaving earlier,' one of them said.

'Yes, I heard you were laid off by the Rajasthan Royals themselves,' said another. That was a code word for our management.

I was evasive. 'Yes, I had to come back to sign something,' I said.

'What did you have to sign?'

Just then the HR team arrived to escort us out. Everyone was smiling, cheerful.

'Let's go to the bar,' one of the laid-off guys said happily. I stayed in the middle of the crowd to escape notice.

'What did you have to sign?' persisted the questioner.

'Some release document. I did not read it.'

We walked past the cars. I could not resist scanning them from the corner of my eye.

'You should not sign any document without reading it.'

There. I saw a guy sitting in the third car holding what could be a camera. I kept my head down and crouched a bit. I should have changed my shirt, I cursed.

Finally the gang went into the bar and I sneaked out. The cars were no longer visible.

Auto-rickshaw to Mylapore then.

∾

It was only when I reached Malini's house that I realized I probably should have called ahead. I had no idea if she would be at home or not.

The house was an independent one in a corner of Mylapore. Small garden. Old building. Father was probably a retired civil servant.

The truth was, I had never talked to girls much in my life. I was a distant admirer. They generally ignored me completely in conversations. The couple of times that I had talked to women of my age, I'd always had panic attacks and stuttered through sentences.

Not the best person to convince a girl to go anywhere.

I opened the compound gate and went in. No dogs. I rang the doorbell.

As I was waiting, I felt a very weird sensation, like someone was standing just behind me and watching me. I turned to look but there was nobody.

I rang the bell again. The feeling persisted. This time I actually felt someone touching my neck. I turned around, scared. Just then, the door opened. I tried to mask my confusion and was not very successful.

'Yes?' asked Malini.

'Hello,' I said and stared.

She was about my height, athletic and attractive. Very attractive.

'Yes?' she repeated, showing a little impatience.

'Hi, Arjun speaking,' I said, in English.

She smiled and said, 'Okay, speak.'

I became more embarrassed and stuttered, 'I . . . I . . . I can come in?'

'No, you can't. What do you want?'

I peered into the house desperately. There was a large portrait of some king visible in the hall.

'L . . . L . . . Looking for the king painting,' I said, and pointed at it.

She looked suspicious. But she also softened because of my stuttering.

'You want to look at that painting?' she asked.

'Yes.'

'Amma . . .' she shouted, turning to look behind her.

Her mother walked into the hall.

'This man wants to see our painting.'

Her mother came closer and asked, 'You saw the magazine feature?'

I nodded vigorously.

'Come in. Malini, get some water.'

I walked in after taking off my shoes. Whoever or whatever was behind, watching me, was still there.

I thought I would sit in the hall, but the mother started walking up the stairs. I followed her. On the first floor, there was a large airy room, with big windows. It had a few paintings. In the middle were a couple of colourful sofas. She asked me to sit on one.

I sat down and remembered that I had to turn on my walkie-talkie. I put my hand in my pocket and pushed some button.

There were four paintings in the hall, all with the same man featured on them. In one, he was carrying a sword, and looking very wild. In all he had a lot of jewellery on and looked quite royal. The paintings were old, but seemed to have been restored in some fashion. Obviously these people or the paintings had been featured in some magazine. Maybe they were important paintings.

Malini came back with water, which I drank eagerly.

Both mother and daughter looked at me expectantly.

'Very nice,' I said.

'Thank you.'

'Great paintings.'

They looked at each other.

'Who painted them? You?' I asked Malini.

It was the wrong thing to say. They seemed annoyed.

'No, it is from Kattabomman Nayakkar's artist.'

Who?

'Okay. Where is he now? He deserves appreciation.'

Another mistake.

'He is dead.'

'Oh, poor man.'

'He has been dead for two hundred years.'

I closed my eyes. Oh, *that* Kattabomman.

One of the earliest fighters against the British in India was a local chieftain near Tirunelveli, named Veerapaandiya Kattabomman. He was brave and the British hanged him near the village of Kayataar for his troubles. So these paintings were done by his court artist. Interesting.

I knew about Kattabomman only because there was a famous Tamil movie by that name. It featured the great Shivaji Ganesan playing the title role.

My walkie-talkie buzzed. Maybe, just maybe, the morons at BSD could have given me some background information. I ignored it.

'Excuse me,' said Malini, 'you are here to see the paintings after reading the magazine, right?'

'Yes.'

'All this was covered in the magazine. How did you miss it?'

'Oh, of course I read it, but I just wanted to be sure.'

The mother went into a room. Maybe she was going to call the police.

I stared at the paintings, searching for something intelligent to say.

'So, this is Kattabomman. He does not look like Shivaji Ganesan,' I said.

'Get up,' Malini said.

'Wha . . . what?'

'Get the hell up. This is not Kattabomman. This is my great-great grandfather, Vellaya Thevar. That was the purpose of the whole magazine feature. You obviously came here for some other reason. Get out.'

Her mother came back from the kitchen carrying an *arivaal* – a sickle.

'What did you think of us? You thought we were defenceless women?' she screamed, waving the *arivaal*.

Of all the people to entangle with, I had chosen the descendants of some martial clan. The mother and daughter could easily beat me up and throw me out of the window.

Just then, we heard the sound of the compound gate being opened.

The main door was closed and Malini went up to the window to see who was coming.

'Amma, there is some big white guy coming in,' she said.

I stiffened. Big Bruce? Here? The guy was like the freaking Terminator.

My walkie-talkie buzzed again. I took it from my pocket and looked at the display.

'Get ready to run,' it said.

The doorbell rang. The mother handed the *arivaal* to Malini and went down to open the door.

We looked at each other in an awkward moment.

I said, 'Look, I came here to ask for your help.'

'You can explain to the police,' she said.

'You have to listen to me. The guy coming upstairs is very dangerous. I came here to save you.'

There were heavy footsteps on the stairs. The mother came in first. She looked pale.

Big Bruce stepped in after her.

He looked strange. His movements were like a robot or a zombie. He came in slowly, with a gun in his hand.

'Hi,' I said.

He ignored me completely.

Instead, he turned towards Malini and said, 'I am from BSD Technologies.' Then he raised his gun at her.

I realized that he had not come for me. He wanted to kill Malini, for some reason. The mother screamed and rushed at him. He tried to push her away. They both scuffled.

I went towards him. He did not even turn. I crashed into him, hoping to topple him over. All that happened was I bounced back a solid two feet, and fell in a heap.

'Run,' I yelled at Malini. She seemed to be trying to attack him with the *arivaal*. The mother had been pushed away and was looking for a weapon. God, what a family.

Bruce raised his gun again. I ran up and kicked him in the back of his leg.

Suddenly he uttered a short scream and buckled down.

I was surprised. Perhaps the back of his leg was his weak point? I had to note that.

But no, he was clutching at his head and rolling around. He crashed into a sofa and then lay still.

We all stared at him. Did he die because I'd kicked him in the leg? Malini looked at me for a second, with what seemed like admiration in her dark eyes. I puffed up. Wow, I had secret powers.

The mother, who obviously had nerves of steel, walked up to Bruce and calmly checked his pulse.

'He is alive,' she announced.

'Yeah, just knocked out,' I said, as if I had put just the right amount of force behind the kick so as to not kill him.

'Who are you? What should we do with him?' Malini asked.

The walkie-talkie crackled.

'Hi,' said Aman.

They both jumped and looked around. I took out the walkie-talkie and waved it in front of them.

'Hi, Malini, I'm Aman, the CFO of BSD Technologies,' Aman said.

'BSD? That is where this person said he was from.'

'Yes, I know. He was lying. But under hypnotic trance. He was hypnotized to say it,' said Aman.

Malini looked confused. 'Who are you people? Why are you here?'

'We'll explain that shortly. But you and your mother should leave your home now. It is not safe for you there.'

'I'm going to call the police,' she said.

'No, please. It may not help you.'

Malini turned to her mother and said, 'Amma, call the police.'

I said into the walkie-talkie, 'Aman, this may be a good time for you to explain.'

'Arjun, please do not interfere. And please get her here. Things are getting very bad with Sathish.'

There came the sound of a police siren.

'Uh, it seems like the police are already here,' I said.

'Leave, then.'

The walkie-talkie cut off.

5

THE RISE OF THE DEMON

I sat in a small room filled with filing cabinets. There were two ancient almirahs overflowing with papers. The desk in the centre had some books and a computer.

A police officer sat behind the computer and stared at me.

This was not what I had imagined an interrogation room would look like. It made me feel a little better, because it would not be easy for the policeman to torture me in this room. The papers would cushion me if he slapped me around. Banging my head on the desk was out of question because the computer hard disk could crash.

The policeman, who introduced himself as Inspector Vishal, had picked us all up at Malini's house and driven straight to the Inspector General's office on Marina Beach Road. We were all now in the Crime Branch department, for some reason; Malini and her mother were in a separate room. Very likely testifying against me.

Big Bruce had been taken to a hospital. He had not yet regained consciousness.

'You are not making sense,' the policeman said. 'You were asked by your company, BSD Technologies, to go get that girl, Malini, for some reason?'

'Yes, Sir.'

'So, you are just doing what you've been told?'

'Correct.'

Another policeman walked in and nodded to Inspector Vishal.

'Okay, here is the thing, Arjun. We called BSD Technologies. We talked to the COO, one Mr Madhan,' the inspector said.

'Okay?'

'He says he has never met you. He denies such a task was ever given to you. He also said you were laid off this afternoon. They have the papers to prove it.'

The policeman left me in the room to think over what he'd just told me.

I realized I was in deep trouble. There was no proof that I worked with the EXM team. I picked up the walkie-talkie from my pocket and pushed the Connect button. Nothing happened. They had really, truly, cut me off.

The bastards.

If Big Bruce never recovered, I could be facing a murder charge. I had also collected ganja that morning, which no one knew about – yet.

I thought about this for some time. Why did the police come to Malini's house? Someone must have tipped them off. Was this whole series of incidents a plot to get me arrested?

I immediately dismissed the idea. I was not that important.

So who had tipped off the police? Why did Bruce say he was from BSD Technologies? Why did Aman say Bruce had been hypnotized? Where was Malini? A look at her face would probably help me recover from this cruel betrayal.

I waited in the room, expecting a hangman to walk in anytime and haul me off.

After letting me stew in suspense for a half hour, Vishal walked in again.

'So, it seems we've got another person from BSD here today,' said Vishal.

Raj!

'He is being investigated in the Cyber Crime department. He has been spinning some story too, it seems, about a top management team. Anyway, we are taking you there.'

Cyber Crime inspector Durai seemed sheepish when we asked him about Raj.

'Yes, we brought him in this morning. But I don't really think he is a bad chap,' Durai said.

'You mean he is innocent?'

'Well, I don't know about that,' he said.

Coming from a policeman, this was surprising.

'Let's put it this way – we've found that he has some talent.'

The Crime Branch inspector seemed mystified.

'Many of the people we arrest may have talents, Durai.'

'Yes, but we decided to use this person's talent.'

Vishal threw up his hands.

'Did you investigate him at all?'

Durai looked even more embarrassed.

'Listen, here is the thing. We have a hacker group who has been mounting attacks against internal systems for the past two weeks. We have not been able to track them. Our man, Raj, seems willing and able to help.'

'So, where is he? Did you let him go?'

'No, of course not. He is in the Lab, helping us fight crime.'

Vishal glared at Durai.

'We have no funds, man. This guy said he'll work for free. And he is super smart.'

'Okay, can we talk to him?'

'Sure, you can take the room,' Durai said and left.

Raj was all smiles when he walked in a few minutes later. He seemed surprised to see me.

'Yo,' he waved, taking no notice of Vishal.

'Hi Raj.'

'Sit down,' said Vishal. He then leaned on his elbows and stared at Raj for a minute.

'Do you know this man?' he then asked, pointing at me.

'Yes, Sir. He is my colleague.'

'I see. Was he laid off today?'

'No, Sir. He works with the EXM team.'

Vishal sat back and stared at the ceiling for some time.

'Listen, guys, if you tell me the truth, I do not have to break every bone in your body.'

We remained silent.

'Now, Raj, why did you hack into BSD's systems?'

'They are easy to hack,' responded Raj.

'So you admit to hacking into the systems?'

'It is not hacking if your root server password is "password",' he said.

'Very funny. We could put you away in jail for some time.'

'Sir, there are far bigger problems than me,' Raj said.

'The EXM team is keeping the CEO confined on the eighth floor; I think they are holding him against his will.'

Vishal stared at the ceiling again. It seemed to be his favourite thinking position.

'Why don't we start from the beginning,' he said.

By the time I finished my story it was four in the evening. I left out my ganja quest and simply emphasized the secretive behaviour and the mysterious happenings on the eighth floor.

'There is someone there and I think his name is Sathish. Circumstantial evidence leads us to conclude that it must be the CEO,' I said as if I were Sherlock Holmes.

Raj nodded. 'I found their documents and accounts. It says they're paying some sorcerer to lay charms and things like that – I guess it's some kind of code. They're taking over the company by hiding the CEO,' he said.

'What do you mean sorcerer?'

'Like the guys who invoke spirits.'

Vishal looked disbelieving.

'I can show you the documents. I've copied them on my server.'

Raj used a server run from his home for all his hacking-related documents.

'No, wait,' said Vishal.

Raj continued. 'It says this sorcerer is invoking some ancient spirit, someone who died two hundred years back. The EXM team is involved in exorcism, is what the document says.'

I sat up.

'Whose spirit?'

'Enough spirit talk,' said Vishal.

'But, Sir, this may be important. Which spirit are they talking about?'

'Some general from Tirunelveli. Some Thevar,' said Raj.

'Is it Vellaya Thevar?'

'Could be . . .' said Raj.

'Shut up,' said the inspector.

I was only happy to. So, Malini's ancestor was being invoked by some sorcerer. Raj seemed to think the EXM documents were coded and contained some secret message. Maybe there was none. Maybe they really were talking about exorcism, not company restructuring. Is that why they wanted me to get Malini? To help in the exorcism?

It seemed to me the whole top management of BSD had gone crazy or were involved in some cult.

Vishal spread his hands on the table.

'Guys, I am the investigator in charge of finding Sathish Kumar, based on a police complaint. The complaint was made last week, by someone called Kevin Anderson, in Chennai. Otherwise, none of us want to be involved in this. This Anderson person has been applying pressure on us from a higher level. He is an American and I am not sure what his interest in this could be.'

'Is he from PH Capital?' I asked.

'Could be. No idea. Usually only minimum information reaches the investigator. It is like a stupid game,' said Vishal. 'Anyway, this Anderson person wants to find out where Sathish is. Surprisingly, BSD Technologies themselves do not seem to care about his whereabouts. They have been giving out standard press releases, which makes the whole thing suspicious.'

'Sathish is on the eighth floor, I'm sure,' said Raj.

'Okay, but what about this guy who came to kill the girl?'

'Maybe BSD sent him to kill the girl because she knows something.'

'Then why send me?' I asked.

'Yes, the whole setup does not make sense. We're missing something.'

'Sir, may I ask you something?' I said.

'Yes?'

'How did you arrive at Malini's house so fast? Who tipped you?'

'I received an anonymous call at one o'clock. The caller said I would learn something about Sathish at that address. I never expected a murder attempt.'

We all stared at the ceiling now.

Finally, Raj said, 'Can I go back to my team? I have work to do.'

'This is not your team. You do not work here. We are the police department. You are a criminal,' said Vishal.

His cell phone rang and he left the room to take the call.

I turned to Raj. 'So, Raj, you are catching hackers now?'

'I plan to get a job here. The inspector made me an offer.'

I whistled.

'By the way, Arjun, this case with BSD is a very strange business. You have to take it seriously.'

'Listen, you have not seen that guy Bruce. Any business that involves him, in any part, is taken seriously.'

'How is the girl?'

Vishal walked in before I could answer. He seemed harried. He sat down and stared at the ceiling some more.

'So, Arjun, we are going to trap these guys at BSD,' he said suddenly.

'*We*, Sir?'

He smiled.

'Yes, unlike your last team, you can trust the police department.'

I was not sure about this.

He looked at his watch.

'Let's leave now. I've asked Malini to join us.'

'Where are we are going?' I asked

'To rescue Sathish,' he said, clapping his hands.

I sat with Malini in the back of an unmarked police car. Vishal and Raj were in the front.

Vishal had described his plan to us. He wanted to go into BSD, pretending to be Malini's relative or escort. After gaining entry to the eighth floor, he would open the door to the adjoining room and confirm Sathish's presence. However, he had no specific idea on how exactly he would do this.

I did not like the plan. I wanted Malini to be safe somewhere, instead of walking into BSD and palling around with cultish people. She was being used as bait so BSD would open the doors to us.

I suggested that she should be kept out of the plan, but Malini seemed to think this was a lovely adventure, so, here we were, in the back of the car.

I thought of communicating with her somehow. I could remember her cell phone number and Vishal had given me a temporary, crappy cell phone for use in the 'operation'.

I took out the phone and typed a text message: *Hi, Arjun here.*

Her phone buzzed. She took it out and looked at the message. Then she looked at me. I pointed at the phone.

What's up? she messaged back.
You are in great danger.
She smiled.
Yes, exciting, right?
Who is Vellaya Thevar?
She frowned.
My great-great grandfather.
Do you know of any sorcerer?
She frowned again.
No.
It seems BSD has a doc that says they hired a sorcerer to call Mr Vellaya Thevar back.

Malini giggled when she read that message. 'What is it?' Vishal asked.

'Nothing.'

The car moved slowly in peak traffic. It was half past five and we were stuck near Adyar Bridge.

At least half an hour more to reach BSD.

I went back to the phone.

This Vellaya Thevar – good man? I typed.

Yes. Fought against British.

Is there anyone else named Vellaya Thevar in your family now?

Yes. Many small Vellaya Thevars running around. Almost every male child is named Vellaya Thevar.

Oh.

This complicated things. Could the EXM team be talking about an actual living member of her family, with the same name?

I wanted to talk about other things, maybe flirt a bit. But all this Thevar talk discouraged me somewhat.

The Thevars are a martial caste in south Tamil Nadu. They were the primary warriors for the Pandya kingdom, which ruled from Madurai. They spent two thousand years fighting various other clans and amidst themselves.

Then modernity came and they all had to become policemen or take up other jobs. All their two thousand-year fighting instincts were kept suppressed to be released on one and only one occasion: when their daughters were wooed by 'undesirables'. They kept their *arivaals* sharpened for that purpose.

This was true for all Thevars and must be doubly true for the descendants of some guy who fought with Kattabomman.

'Let us go over the plan again,' Vishal said.

ॐ

We parked outside BSD. Raj stayed in the car with a policeman; Vishal, Malini and I went up to the security gate.

'Can you call Dileepan?' I said to the guard. 'Tell him this is Arjun with Malini.'

We waited while the security guard made the call. There was a camera above the gate. Perhaps Dileepan could see us.

The guard waved us in.

'Wait in the reception,' he said.

We went into the building. There was another camera at the reception. I glanced at Malini. She did not even seem to be nervous. I was ready to run to the bathroom.

The lift doors opened and Dileepan walked out with two guards.

He had, of course, seen Vishal through the camera. The guards stood by the lift, while he walked up to us.

'Arjun, what a surprise,' he said.

'This is Malini,' I said.

'Yes, of course. Very happy you could come.'

He looked at Vishal expectantly.

'I am Malini's cousin,' said Vishal.

'I see. Okay, why don't you stay here. Arjun and Malini, come with me,' he said and turned to go.

'I'm sorry, but I need to come with you,' Vishal said.

Dileepan looked annoyed.

'We won't eat your cousin,' he said.

'My family and Malini's mother asked me to accompany her.'

Malini piped in then. 'I'm not going without my cousin.'

Dileepan looked at her for a couple of seconds, and then walked a few steps away, pulled out his walkie-talkie and started whispering into it, covering his mouth too, as if we would lip-read.

After a couple of minutes, he switched it off and came back.

'What is your name?' he asked Vishal.

'Nathan.'

'Okay, you can come up. But if you create any problems, I will have to call the police commissioner's office. I know people there,' Dileepan said sternly.

I struggled to keep a straight face.

On the seventh floor we got out of the lift and did the same walk I had done twice earlier that day. I couldn't spot any gun barrels pointing at us though, and the place looked tidier. Someone had tried to cover the bullet holes as well. Dileepan keyed in the password and we went up the stairs to the eighth floor.

'Stay here,' Dileepan said and went into the conference room.

There was complete silence in the corridor outside. No clanking chains, nothing. It was very quiet.

'It will be very disappointing if Sathish is not here,' I said.

'Disappointment is an understatement, since you will be in jail,' Vishal said.

Dileepan came out and said, 'Malini and Arjun, you can come in. Nathan, I will take you to the lounge.'

At first Vishal did not seem to remember that he was Nathan. Then he followed Dileepan. This was surprising because I assumed he would want to come in with us. Perhaps he had other plans.

I opened the door and went into the conference room with Malini.

It was hot in the room. The table was piled with papers. The three people in there, Madhan, Keerthi and Aman, looked older than they had that morning.

'Here's Malini,' I said dramatically.

Aman waved. Madhan and Keerthi broke into a smile.

'Hello,' said Malini.

'Thank God you came,' Keerthi said.

'We have no time. Can you help us?' Aman said.

'What do you want me to do?'

Aman was about to answer when there was a bloodcurdling roar from the next room. Something hit the wall hard. Malini stepped back in fear.

'Let's go,' Aman said. 'We can't control him any longer.' They all got up.

Vishal stepped into the room. He had a gun in his hand. 'Nobody move,' he said.

Then he turned to Malini and said, 'You can go back down. It is too dangerous here.'

'Who are you?' Aman asked.

'Inspector Vishal, Crime Branch. By the way, your man, what's-his-name, is under arrest for trying to hit a police officer.'

Ah . . . so Dileepan had got his butt kicked.

As Malini left the room, Aman said, 'Inspector, you are making a mistake.'

'I need to see the person you have confined in the next room.'

'Nobody is being confined,' said Aman. The clanking sound resumed.

'Open that door,' Vishal ordered.

Aman looked around for support. Then he gave up and walked to his right. He stuck a key that he pulled out from his pocket into the door's keyhole.

He then turned and said to Vishal, 'Can I explain?'

'No. Open the damn door.'

There was silence now, from the other room. The key was turned and the door opened.

Vishal walked towards the room and peered in. I followed him. It was dark inside and the smell of urine wafted out. Keerthi backed away as far as possible.

At first it seemed as if no one was there. Then as our eyes got used to the darkness, we could make out a man sitting in the middle of the room. He was staring straight at us. All around him were clumps of some dark substance. In the corner there was a basin. He had a beard and looked at us with very red eyes.

His arms and legs were chained to the floor.

'What the hell is this!' Vishal said.

There was no answer from the other three.

Vishal opened the door wider. 'Mr Sathish?' he asked.

There was no answer from the man. He continued to look at us without blinking. I realized that the dark stuff on the floor was hair. He must have pulled his own hair out.

'Release him from those chains,' Vishal said.

'Oh, no. Bad idea,' Madhan said.

'Release him!' yelled Vishal.

'You'll be harming the entire city. This man is possessed,' Aman said.

'Shut up, and free him.'

Aman took out some keys from his pocket and showed them to Vishal.

'You can do it yourself.'

Vishal took the keys and tossed them to me. The man in the room looked at the keys hungrily.

I did not like this new responsibility. First of all, my hands were shaking and I doubted if I could open any locks. Secondly, the man in the room was now focused on me and the keys.

I stepped into the room and slowly walked towards the man. 'There, there,' I said. 'Everything will be all right.'

When I got closer, he growled. I stood still, staring at him. It was definitely Sathish, our CEO.

Suddenly he lunged at me. I stepped back quickly, but he managed to get one hand on my arm, and I dropped the keys.

'Run!' screamed Aman.

Sathish had grabbed the keys and was now busy freeing himself. I ran back and jumped past Vishal, who yelled, 'All of you, stay here. You are under arrest,' at the general lot of us. The mass arrest order was not working. We all ran for the conference room door. There was a snarl behind us and I scrambled to get out. A wire caught my foot and I kicked at it. Madhan showed his leadership qualities by pushing Keerthi out of his way and running out first. Aman was dashing out with as much dignity as he could muster. Something flew past us and crashed into the opposite wall. I turned and saw that Vishal was the projectile. A gleeful, maniacal laughter rang out. I threw a laptop behind me and jumped out of the conference room. I could see Aman disappearing down the stairs.

I, instead, turned left and flew for the lounge.

I turned the corridor and peeked behind me. Sathish was walking out of the conference room, a gun in his hand.

I was trapped. He could head in my direction and take his time finishing me off. I could be *dead* in five minutes.

I ran to the lounge and opened the door. Dileepan was sitting there on a sofa, nursing his neck. He looked up at me with a vacant stare.

'Sathish is free,' I said.

'Yes, I could hear him here. It's all over.'

I wanted to tell him he needed the 'can-do' spirit, but it was not the right time. I ran past him and looked out the window. It was a sheer drop to the ground. We were trapped.

I waited and listened. There was no sound from outside. As I looked out the window again, the glass just below me shattered and a leather chair flew out.

'He is on the seventh floor,' I said.

Dileepan did not answer.

'How can we control him? With ganja?' I asked.

'No.'

'Should we get a psychiatrist?'

Dileepan laughed drily.

'Yes, offering therapy and counselling to Vellaya Thevar is a great idea.'

I opened the window slightly. I could hear thumping sounds from the floor below us.

'Come on, how can we control him?' I asked again.

He mumbled something.

'What?'

'The girl with you can help.'

Ah . . . Malini. She must be downstairs. I needed to get her.

I fished out the mobile phone from my pocket and called her number while I ran out of the room.

'Where are you?' I asked when she picked up.

'At the reception. What's happening upstairs?'

I ran down the stairs to the seventh floor.

'Sathish is free and he is in a murderous rage.'

'Okay, because I saw some falling furniture. I thought they were re-doing the interiors.'

Funny girl.

'He is coming down,' I said.

'Okay, let me get out of here.'

'No, please listen.'

'Yes?'

'It seems you can calm him down.'

'How?'

'You just stay in the reception and he will come down there. I think he will calm down when he sees you.'

'I see. You know that for sure?'

There was a crashing sound from the phone.

'Hi,' said Malini.

'Yes?' I said pounding down the stairs.

'I saw the people from the conference room just leave. They seem to be in a hurry.'

'Yes, Sathish may be trying to get them.'

'Okay, that sound was a couple of computers being sent after them.'

'Okay,' I said, panting. I was on the third floor now.

'I'm getting out of here,' Malini said.

'Oh no, please stay.'

'I think he is close by,' she said and hung up.

I raced down the stairs and reached the ground floor. And stopped.

The receptionist was lying face down on the floor, her broken computer next to her. The door leading outside was shattered, glass pieces strewn everywhere.

Sathish had gone out into the wide world.

I walked out of BSD slowly. There were people running back and forth on the road. A couple of guys were flailing around on the ground. I could not spot the police car with Raj in it. Traffic had stopped because a motorbike had been thrown down in the middle of the road.

A sense of complete failure overcame me. Whatever I got involved in ended up being a disaster.

We had unleashed a violent mad man on the streets of Chennai.

6

THE EXIM DOCUMENTS

I should have gone home then.

But I remembered that Vishal was lying injured upstairs, and most probably needed medical care.

Several BSD employees were streaming out onto the road. They'd had enough. I could hear an ambulance siren approaching. There were also a couple of television press vans slowing down in front of the building.

The vans decided it for me. A vague suspicion stirred in my mind. I walked back into the BSD building.

On the seventh floor, the vault door was open, as I had left it. I wondered where Dileepan was. Probably taking off with office supplies.

The conference room was a mess. Vishal was still lying in a corner, unconscious. I walked up to him to check how badly injured he was. He had no visible wounds, and was breathing normally.

A Blackberry phone was lying nearby. I picked it up to call his department. They would want to know.

He had new text messages.

I opened the inbox. He should probably password-protect his phone, being a policeman and all, I thought. The last message was from a contact named Anderson. I had heard that name before.

'Thanks for getting him out,' said the message. 'You have been a great help.'

I scrolled down. There were no other messages from Mr Anderson.

I opened the phone's call log and checked his received calls that afternoon. Vishal had received a single call when we were in his office. The log showed that call to be from the same Anderson. He had also called Vishal earlier that day.

Interesting.

So, this person, Anderson, had registered a complaint that Sathish was missing. Then he obviously tipped Vishal off about Big Bruce going to Malini's house. Once Malini and I were in the police station, he used us to free Sathish.

Even though Bruce's attack misfired, Anderson had rallied and accomplished his objective.

Brilliant.

Was he one of the Americans who had threatened me in the Guindy forest? Was he was their leader?

Worthy adversary.

I got up and walked to the window.

Traffic was entirely static as far as I could see.

Perhaps I should take a stab at unwinding this mess, I thought. My job was gone – BSD was finished as a company. It would be interesting to find out why this had happened. It all started with Sathish's collapse at NASSCOM, one month back. Or did it start much earlier? It is hard in a corporate culture to know if your CEO is stark raving mad or a genius. Maybe he had been crazy all this time.

It was getting dark. I turned and looked through the

open door to the next room. It seemed ominous. Full of menace.

Aman's laptop was open. It had not fallen off the table. And it had not been locked.

∽

Raj had said he had copied the EXM documents to his server at home. He had given me access to the server some time back.

I went to Remote Desktop and connected to his computer. In the data drive, there was a document dump with hundreds of folders, including one named 'EXM'. I opened it. There were only three documents. One was a Microsoft Word file named 'EXM Mission' – probably the vision and scope statement. The second was an Excel file called 'ActivityLog'. The third was the project plan I had seen that morning.

I opened the 'EXM Mission' document. Glanced at Vishal. He was still out. I had no desire to help him.

Chennai

15 Oct 2012

The EXM Team Vision

IN ORDER THAT BSD Technologies may take on the might of former clients and Hedge Fund giant, PH Capital, headquartered in New York City.

IN ORDER THAT we may negotiate a solution to our violation of the non-disclosure contract with PH.

TO DISCLOSE IF necessary, acting on MORAL values, the data currently encrypted with WikiLeaks, as wished by Mr Sathish Kumar, our unmatched LEADER.

TO PRESERVE the credibility of our organization and that of Mr Sathish Kumar, in light of the above DISCLOSURE.

WE, THE EXM OPERATION, SHALL:

```
FREE THE LEADER from the clutches of the terrible
demon, protector of the World of Ahi, the unassailable
VELLAYA THEVAN.
    RETRIEVE ON HIS WISHES the incriminating DATA on PH
Capital.
    PUBLISH AND EXPOSE to the world, the machinations of
PH Capital.
    FREE! RETRIEVE! PUBLISH! EXPOSE!
    WE SWEAR REVENGE!!!
```

The document read like something written by the hacker group Anonymous, not by a bunch of MBAs. Maybe these guys were helping themselves to a little bit of the ganja.

I opened the activity log. It was authored by Aman. I scanned it quickly. There were long lists of tasks every day, but most were notes on payments.

15 Oct 2012 – Strategized on vision and process for EXM

16 Oct 2012 – Skype conference with Mr Kevin Anderson. Mr Anderson refused our offer

16 Oct 2012 – Paid for office space and holding room in corporate office. Receipt in file.

17 Oct 2012 – One Mr Bruce caused injury to Mr Madhan. Doctor charges.

17 Oct 2012 – Hired security firm Black Guards. Receipt for advance in file.

18 Oct 2012 – Sathish located.

20 Oct 2012 – Paid Mr Idumban Kaari, freelance sorcerer, opening advance.

And so on. A few entries caught my attention.

31 Oct 2012 – Sathish secured with Mr Idumban's help. Paid him. No receipt.

03 Nov 2012 – Commissioned search for very low-level EXM resource.

Hmm . . . that could be me. Yes, it was.

05 Nov 2012 – Identified one Mr Arjun Palani based on criteria. Checked with Mr Idumban. Cleared for offering.

06 Nov 2012 – Mr Idumban presented first plan for approaching Vellaya Thevan. Involved some sacrifices.

06 Nov 2012 – Paid Mr Idumban for profile of Vellaya Thevan and his location in time (Note: 1800 AD, two hundred years in Ahi Loka)

07 Nov 2012 – Attacked today by PHC for freeing Sathish. Attack repulsed by the Black Guards team. Paid for hospital and ammunition charges.

08 Nov 2012 – First review of project plan with Mr Idumban. Date identified for EXM – 13th Friday.

Interesting. Obviously this Idumban Kaari was someone they trusted. Was he really a sorcerer or was that the new name they now gave corporate consultants?

I checked Aman's Skype account. It did have a contact named Idumban Kaari. It was a Skype Out contact, a mobile phone number.

I first noted the number in my police-issue mobile phone. Then I took a headset lying nearby, put it on and dialled the number on Skype.

After a few rings, the phone was picked up, and a deep voice said, 'Idumban.'

There were wild screams in the background. He sounded like he was in a discotheque.

'Sir, this is Arjun Palani.'

There was silence on the other end. Silence from Idumban, that is. The wild screams were still going on.

'Who?'

'Arjun. Arjun Palani, with BSD Technologies,' I yelled into the phone.

'Yes, okay.'

'Sir, Sathish has escaped. He is in the city.'

'Okay.'

'Can you help me get him under control?'

'Where is Aman?' he yelled above the cacophony in the background.

'I don't know. It is just me here, now.'

'Okay, thing is . . .' he hesitated, 'I am in the middle of an exorcism here. It is a particularly tricky case. Can you call me later?'

'Sir, that may be too late. Can you tell me where you think Sathish might be and how we can control him?'

Idumban turned and yelled something, probably to the victim. The screaming stopped and was replaced by a low humming.

'You want to know where Sathish is in this world?'

'What other world? Yes, of course.'

'Okay, I have no idea where he is.'

Nice. This guy was a big help.

'How can I locate him?'

'I do not know. I can only think of one thing.'

'Yes?'

'Their goal is to destroy Sathish's reputation, credibility, in the public eye.'

'Okay?'

'That is all. That is why they are using the demon. Maybe you can find him using that information.'

'What? How the hell am I . . .'

Over the last few seconds the humming had been growing louder. Now, there was a crashing sound from the other end. I could hear Idumban cursing and the phone cut off.

I banged the table. God, how was I going to solve this problem?

I stared at the vision statement.

TO PRESERVE the credibility of our organization and that of Mr Sathish Kumar.

I got up and walked to the white board at one end of the wall. I picked up a marker and wrote:

October 1 – Sathish goes crazy in NASSCOM conference

October 15 – EXM team formation

October to November – Attempts by Anderson (PH Capital?) to free Sathish

November 13 – Sathish freed

I stared at the sequence for some time.

To preserve the credibility . . .

So, PH Capital was trying to destroy Sathish's credibility for some reason. Now he was free. But their goal would not be accomplished just by setting him free. It was possible that the mayhem on the road outside would never be connected with Sathish. Unless the television cameras caught him. Even then, it was pretty difficult to recognize Sathish, in his current state.

The best thing Anderson could do was to get Sathish in front of a television camera, and make sure he was recognized by people.

Now that I thought about it, Sathish's antics at the NASSCOM conference probably had the same purpose – to destroy his credibility at a high-profile venue.

In a flash, I realized where Sathish would be.

7

THE TRADE CENTRE

I ran out of the BSD office, fishing for my phone. 'Auto,' I screamed.

Traffic had cleared up completely. An auto-rickshaw came straight for me and screeched to a halt two feet away.

'Chennai Trade Centre,' I said, and jumped in.

'Raj,' I said into the phone.

'Hi, man.'

'Raj, can you contact Malini?'

'She is right here, with me.'

I paused.

'Where are you?'

'Coffee Day in Adyar.'

I felt a pang of jealousy.

'We're celebrating our narrow escape from our beloved CEO.'

'I see. Can you get her and come to the Trade Centre? I think Sathish is going to be there.'

'That sounds like a good reason to not go there,' he said.

'No, come on. Malini can help him.'

Malini was laughing about something in the background.

'Okay, but we just ordered more coffee.'

'Forget the damn coffee. Leave now.'

I hung up. I had to contact Aman and the rest of the EXM team.

The Trade Centre was a few miles to the northwest of the BSD offices. They were currently holding an exhibition by software vendors. Friday and Saturday were the final days of the exhibition, and the chief minister was supposed to attend. All the industry bigwigs would be there. Along with the media.

I was pretty sure Anderson would have Sathish show up there, if they could control him.

The auto weaved its way through the evening rush hour.

I picked up the walkie-talkie from my pocket and pushed the Connect button.

'Hello, Aman . . . anyone?'

There was silence. Then I heard a voice, with no accent.

'Hello Mr Arjun.'

I was silent.

There was a soft chuckle from the other end.

'Thanks for all your help,' the American said.

Lilting music came floating from the other end of the line, along with distant laughter.

I cut the connection.

So, Aman had been caught.

I had to manage Sathish myself.

At the Trade Centre I learnt that the executives of some fifty different technology companies were assembled in a smaller conference hall. They were being addressed by Muthiah, a 'Technology Evangelist'.

All the media was there.

The media loved Muthiah. Most programmers, like me,

hated him. He was the guy who gave managers weird ideas, such as playing team sports in the middle of a project.

Muthiah's lectures were usually featured on business channels. He said he had come up with the problem plaguing IT companies in India: it was not the recession, not the global economic downturn, or even 'delayed labour reform'. No. The problem was – lack of correct breathing by managers.

Yes. Business managers were all breathing wrong.

Apparently he had studied a bunch of them – probably by standing really close to them – and figured this out. They were all flexing their neck incorrectly, and breathing like horses.

Instead, he said, they should take his breathing and motivational therapy classes – for only twenty thousand rupees a month.

If all our managers were getting their breathing wrong – this most basic activity – then I did not understand how they could manage giant corporations.

Over time, Muthiah had made a fortune teaching correct breathing; he had also diversified into other areas that managers got wrong. They all flocked to his sermons to hear what they had messed up now.

I could have told them for free.

The Centre was crowded with people attending the exhibition. I scoped out the hall. I had been there before, for a technology seminar. It would be a great place to release Sathish. The entry could be arranged, I was sure. The guy at the door looked positively eager to let people in for an 'allowance'.

I'd heard that the chief minister was coming the next day and could see that there was some security around.

I messaged Raj again, and got a response that was irritating. Apparently they were shopping in some mall on the way. This was not a good sign. Raj was moving in on my girl.

I took a walk around, to see if Anderson and his team were already there. I had realized that he would definitely not expect me at the Trade Centre. The element of surprise was on my side. I intended to keep it that way. I skulked around for some time, but did not see any suspicious activity. Where were they? If Anderson's team arrived with Sathish, the best place to get him in was through the main door to the conference hall. I positioned myself a little way off, in the lobby, pretending to look at some displays.

I saw Malini and Raj walking towards me across the lobby. She was laughing at something Raj had said. After all this was over, I would have to kill Raj.

'They should be bringing Sathish here any time now,' I said.

'Your loyalty knows no bounds,' Raj said.

'Why aren't you back at the police station, betraying your former soul mates?' I asked.

Malini stepped in.

'Forgive me, but why are we trying to get in the way of this crazy guy?'

'Malini, you can stop him.'

'How do you figure that?' she said.

'That is why they were trying to kill you,' I said, in a flash of inspiration. 'They were trying to prevent you from controlling Sathish.'

Was that true? Who knew? They had made sure the ganja did not work. Killing Malini would have eliminated another way to control Sathish.

While we were talking, I kept scanning the lobby and the entrance, watching for Sathish.

'What should I do?' asked Malini.

'Go to the conference hall,' I said. 'I think they might take him there. And if he comes in, get near him.'

Raj rolled his eyes, and said, 'You understand this could all be an elaborate plot by marketing to enhance brand value?'

∾

They both headed to the entrance of the conference hall as I walked outside the building and stood by a pillar.

A bunch of men in suits went past me. My phone buzzed.

Raj had sent a message: 'You can relax. Sathish will not be a problem here.'

I wondered what he meant.

I also wondered if I had made a mistake. Maybe they were not coming here at all.

The hall door opened to let in the men in the suits.

A sound of raucous music and screaming came floating out. I recognized the music. I had heard it half an hour earlier, when Anderson picked up my call to Aman.

Was Sathish already in the hall?

How could that be? He would have created mayhem by now.

I realized that I was picturing him the same way as when I saw him, that evening. But, if Anderson was able to control him, they obviously had other means of getting him to obey them. I remembered the Google link about ganja and controlling victims of possession.

It was in Anderson's interest that Sathish behaved like a time bomb. Get into the hall, let everyone see him and recognize him. And then have him behave crazy.

In that case, Sathish must already be in there. I must have missed him because I expected a slavering crazy man. He was now a slavering crazy man in a suit. Who would be at home with other executives.

I turned and ran for the hall entrance, and then decided I needed a better view. There were stairs going up to the left, probably to a higher floor or balcony. I changed direction and sprinted up the stairs.

There was a door on the first floor, but I realized that was the mezzanine. I was about to open the door. Then I stopped.

Anderson's team could be in there. What better place to monitor the whole hall?

I hesitated.

What was the hall layout like? There were probably other balconies.

And then there was the stage.

I walked downstairs slowly and went around the corridor. There were cables trailing at the far end. That must be the media, scrounging for extra power.

I walked to the other end of the corridor. The music and screaming got louder. The cables went into the hall through a door that stood ajar. I opened it and went in.

I was not prepared for the spectacle inside. The media were spread out on the first level below the stage. Their bright lights were all over the hall. On the stage, there was a lone man, standing in front of a mike. He was screaming into the mike, something about letting the past go.

The hall itself was filled with around two hundred executives, standing up and dancing. Many of them had their suit jackets off.

'Innovation, innovation, innovation . . .' screamed Muthiah.

'Innovation, innovation . . .' chanted the crowd.

'Leadership, leadership . . .' he yelled.

The crowd seemed positively delirious.

I had watched a Christian 'tent revival' once on television. This looked like that, only far louder.

'Gentlemen, gentlemen,' Muthiah said. 'You are not yet letting the baggage go. LET IT GO. Take off your ties, unbutton your shirts and throw off the baggage.'

The crowd roared, and I saw several of them struggling with their ties. Some had proceeded to unbutton their shirts. The last thing I needed tonight was to see middle-aged male executives with their beer paunches jiggling around.

Anderson had made a huge mistake, if this was where he had brought Sathish. Muthiah's lectures were exorcisms themselves. A crazy person may not even be noticed here.

I remained in the dark and scanned the balconies. I could not see anybody familiar there.

Then I climbed on top of a small speaker box, still in the dark, and looked carefully at the crowd.

Everywhere I saw the uplifting sight of Indian IT leadership trying to loosen up. In a far corner, I saw Malini and Raj.

I texted Raj: 'Can you see Sathish?'

The response came: 'Near the centre.'

I turned around and peered at the centre of the hall.

There, amidst all the dancing, sat a lone figure at a table. His head was bent down.

I started moving toward him.

Getting to Sathish was difficult. The executives were now positively randy. I saw a couple of them using the opportunity to hug each other. A little bit of cuddling seemed to be going on.

'I see some of you are still not relaxed enough,' Muthiah was saying.

I stopped. If he was talking about Sathish, sitting stationary in the middle, this was a bad idea.

'Get up, get up,' screamed Muthiah. I pushed people away and ran for the centre of the hall. Some of the managers were coaxing a few reticent men out of their jackets.

'You in the middle!' yelled Muthiah. 'Embrace your crazy side!'

Uh-oh.

I was close to Sathish's table now and the people around the table were looking at him.

'What is his name?' yelled Muthiah. 'Get up, let yourself go.'

Someone put his hand on Sathish's shoulder and shook him.

I was now very close to him. I could see that Malini was also trying to get through.

Sathish looked up slowly.

He was clean-shaven and was wearing a nice fitting suit. They had prepared him for the occasion. His eyes were still bloodshot though, and as he looked around, people close to him stepped away.

I yelled, 'Sathish, look here, man!' and tried to point to Malini.

Sathish shook his head and got up. Whatever they had given him to calm down seemed to have gone.

Muthiah shouted, 'Yes, that is it. Step forward.'

Sathish uttered a wild roar.

The crowd close to him cheered.

He roared again, and jumped up on the table. People backed away.

Muthiah probably did not expect this. But he rallied nicely, while the video cameras swung towards Sathish.

'YES!' screamed Muthiah. 'Look at that man. He is a leader.'

Others looked enviously at Sathish. A couple of copycats clambered on top of tables.

Malini came near me and said, 'How do I control him?'

I had no idea. I had assumed that her mere presence would calm him. But it did not seem to be working.

'What is Plan B?' asked Raj.

I had no plan B.

Sathish roared again and launched himself straight into the middle of the crowd around him.

People scattered away and a couple of them screamed. I stepped forward and caught a flash of something.

He had a knife in his hand.

He waved the knife around now. As he tried to launch at people again, Malini walked in front of him.

Sathish crashed straight into her and both of them went down.

'Hey!' I yelled and tried to pull him away. He got up. The knife was still in his hand, and there was blood on it.

A few people screamed and started running for the door.

Sathish stared at the blood; looked at Malini again.

Then he collapsed in my arms.

∽

Raj bent down to look at her. Malini moved. She extended her right arm.

Raj caught her arm and pulled her up.

Her left arm had been cut. There was blood on the floor and on her clothes.

He supported her and looked around.

At that moment, I felt a dizzy spell hit me. The whole hall seemed to swim before my eyes.

It was not just me though. Raj stumbled too, and the people around us grabbed tables and chairs for support. There were more screams.

'Earthquake,' shouted someone. There was a stampede for the doors.

I signalled to Raj and moved towards the side door through which I had come. The media guys were unfazed by the quake, and continued to film the stampede. Muthiah had disappeared from the stage.

Nobody even glanced at us as we snuck out the door, I pulling Sathish along, Malini walking by herself, but leaning on Raj.

We came out into the corridor and followed it around the building. At the back, there was a door leading out and we stumbled out that way. I lay Sathish on the steps and Malini sat down.

'We really did not need an earthquake at this time,' said Raj.

'What earthquake?' said Malini.

I nodded. 'I don't think it was a geographical quake,' I said.

Malini was looking at her left arm. The blood had dried a little bit. She took her dupatta and tried to wrap it around the wound with one hand.

'Here, let me help,' Raj said.

I watched as he tied the dupatta around her arm. She was smiling.

∾

'What do we do now?' Raj said.

'And what if this guy wakes up again?' Malini asked.

'We let him cut you again. Only way to control him,' I said.

'You may need to go see a doctor. Just by the way,' Raj said.

Malini did not seem to care. 'It's not a deep wound. I've had worse in my home town,' she said. I remembered that she was from the warrior clan.

'We have to call the sorcerer,' I said.

It was half-past eight now. I hoped Idumban would have finished dealing with his 'patient'.

He picked up the call on the first ring.

'Hi,' he said in his deep voice.

'I have Sathish with me,' I said. 'And the girl.'

There was a pause.

'You did this by yourself?'

'With some help.'

He chuckled. 'To see that you have been more valuable to this job than the others – it's ironic.'

'What do we do with Sathish?' I said.

'Explain to me exactly how you got him.'

I quickly related what had happened.

'So, he cut her and fell down?'

'Yes.'

'This is not good. It is not good for Sathish. He is in big trouble,' said Idumban.

'Okay.'

'But he has just received the mental equivalent of a punch from Mohammed Ali. He will be out for some time. Can you get the girl to stick with you for some time? She may well be crucial in controlling Sathish tonight.'

'How much time do we have?'

'I was coming to that. We need to arrange the expedition at around three in the morning. Aman and the others have to be there on the trip.'

'What trip?'

'The trip to Ahi,' he said impatiently. 'Listen, there is a lot of ground to cover. The first thing you have to do is get Aman and Madhan. Where are they?'

'I think they are with Anderson.'

'Oh,' he said. There was a pause.

'Is he holding them hostage?' I asked.

'No. I think he will try to make them as crazy as Sathish. Can you get them?'

Sure; I could walk over to Anderson and ask him to release my managers.

'Try to get Aman. He is a good man,' Idumban said, and hung up.

$$\backsim$$

I turned to look at Sathish. He hadn't moved at all.

'Malini, you have to go back home,' I said.

'Thank you for your orders, but no.'

'The sorcerer wants you to stay. It is in our interest for you to stay. But, believe me,' I said, 'you shouldn't be running around with us so late at night.'

'It *is* late,' Raj put in.

'I don't think I'm safe at home. From your conversation,

it seems you know more than I do. Can you tell me why people are trying to kill me?'

I sat down on the steps.

'I don't know the full picture myself,' I said. 'We have an antagonist, a man from PH Capital, I think. They called him a mercenary. His name is Anderson, and he is acting on behalf of his company. We just made him very angry.'

'Why are they trying to kill me?'

'I think you have some power over Sathish, but they cannot just kill you because Vellaya Thevar protects you. I think that is why they had to hypnotize Bruce, the giant who came to your home – so he wouldn't back out.'

'Not a very powerful demon then,' Raj said

'Hey, that's my grandfather you're talking about.'

'Hold on,' I said. 'I need to think. I have to find the people who got us into this mess. I need to get Aman.'

'You know, sorry that we are disturbing your thinking, but you don't have to carry this whole burden by yourself. We could probably help you,' Malini said.

'Yes, we are not feeble minded,' Raj added.

'And I am a political science major. This situation is tailor-made for my area of expertise,' Malini said.

I looked at them for a couple of seconds and then nodded. 'Okay, first we need to find transport. We can't stay here.'

'My car is waiting outside,' Raj said.

'Your car?'

'Yes. I convinced the policeman driving us this afternoon to take us around. He thinks we're on official business.'

I laughed. 'Where is he?'

8

LOCATING MR ANDERSON

We pulled out of the Trade Centre in the middle of the weekend traffic, complete with ear-splitting honks, screeching tires and exhaust fumes.

Sathish was in the back, sleeping like a baby. Malini and Raj were next to him; I sat in front with the driver.

'Do you know where Ahi is?' I asked Raj.

'Is it a place? Town?'

'I don't know ... it seems Aman and the team are supposed to take a trip there at midnight.'

'Let me google it,' Raj said.

The driver spoke up suddenly.

'Raj sir, did you ask that car to follow us?'

Raj looked up.

'Which car?'

'The car with the white guys? One of them has a gun,' he said.

All of us turned to look behind.

The driver said, 'Now he is aiming the gun at us.'

BOOM – the rear window shattered. We all ducked down.

The policeman continued to drive.

'So, not a friend?' he said.

'No.'

'Okay, then.'

He did not attempt to speed up. I peeked behind and took a look. It was a Honda car, and the guys inside were clearly angry.

'Can you try to get away from them?' I said.

'No need sir. Chennai traffic will take care of that.'

I watched as the Honda tried to gain on us. There were auto-rickshaws on either side of it, as well as in front. The auto-rickshaw drivers clearly did not like a mere car trying to pass them.

The Honda driver put his indicator on to switch lanes. This seemed to enrage the other 'proper' drivers further, and they immediately moved to cut him off.

We watched as the driver tried hopelessly to move to either side or in front. He was quickly learning that mad driving skills in New York would not help him in Chennai. The car slowly got swallowed, as if it were sinking in quicksand. There was just a sea of motorbikes and auto-rickshaws now.

It was a sad sight.

'How did they find us?' asked Malini.

'They probably followed us from the Trade Centre,' I said.

'I don't think Ahi is a town, Arjun,' Raj said.

'You could not find anything on it?'

'No. At least not as a physical location.'

I turned to look at him.

'What does that mean?'

'It seems to have some metaphysical meaning.'

'Forget it. Idumban will tell us where it is,' I said.

'Ahi Loka – the world of Ahi. It is a name for the

underworld. Mentioned in the Vedas. Also called Vritra Loka.'

'That does not make any sense,' I said.

'It is the land of no return. Sunk deep down in gloom and darkness, beneath the three earths,' Raj said.

'You can stop now.'

'Let me read further. It is a joyless place of endless caverns filled with the loud ring of pressing-stones; and a place of destruction where the wicked are ground, pierced, boiled, burned, slain, and destroyed. Those found in hell are the fiend and his minions; fools, the voracious, treacherous, and evil, as well as those who make false accusations, who destroy the simple, harm the righteous, worship false gods, and speak untruly.'

'Sounds like any IT company,' I said.

'It is in the Vedas, man. Completely dependable, written by stoned rishis.'

∾

The traffic thinned out as we made for the IT Corridor.

Between TIDEL Park in Adyar and the main IT Corridor in Chennai, a small road cuts to the right. It runs behind the IIT campus. Along that road, walking distance from TIDEL, there is an office complex called Ascendas. Ascendas boasts of a huge food court, and a few offshore development centres.

Next to Ascendas is a small coffee and snacks joint – Aachi's Dosa Shop. This place attracts a sad mix of programmers every Friday night. There is no alcohol, and the whole place reeks of pathos. Clumps of these sad excuses for human beings sit around and discuss the week's happenings – usually complaints about heartless managers, unreasonable clients, psychopathic HR and such cheery oppressors of the technical community.

Sometime back a bright HR guy had come up with an idea to organize 'user group' conferences there. A bunch of HR executives sneaked in and tried to promote 'positive attitudes' and a 'can-do spirit'. They were met with a near riot and were almost ripped limb to limb. The programmers would not stand for their last remaining refuge to be desecrated thus.

We had stopped our car outside Aachi's, and were having a small debate about whether or not to take Sathish in. He was unconscious, but moaning; he sounded delirious. He would not be out of place in Aachi's on a Friday night.

Finally we propped him up and got him to walk while we supported him. Strangely, he could walk with us, almost like a sleep-walker.

We went into Aachi's. People looked at Sathish sympathetically as we passed their tables. They must have thought he was another developer passed out from exhaustion.

We went to a cosy round sofa in a far corner and sat down. Sathish collapsed on the table and continued to sleep.

We ordered a few dosas.

Raj rubbed his eyes and said, 'What now?'

'We have to locate Anderson's base,' I said.

'Hold on,' Malini said, 'we just got shot at. Does that usually happen with you guys?'

'Not me,' I said.

'Never been shot at,' confirmed Raj.

'I don't see any reaction from you ... how about some shock? Some fear?'

We thought about this.

'Hmm . . . no,' I said.

'You know I am a political science major, right? We have psychology as a minor. This is not normal, for human beings.'

Raj drank some water, putting it down as if he were drinking strong liquor. Then he looked up at her and said with an air of profound wisdom, 'You have no idea, do you?'

'About what?'

'We are not normal human beings. We are computer programmers.'

She smiled. She looked even more radiant when she smiled.

'That makes you special?'

'That plus the pressure of being India's engines for growth. Without us,' he gestured around, 'there would be no Ascendas. Hell, there would be no IT Corridor.'

'Pretty humble of you.'

'We are men of steel. Hearts of iron. Unsung heroes of the digital age.'

'I don't know about that,' I said, 'but what I have been doing since morning beats cubicle death. I am having way more fun.'

'Fun that could kill you?' she asked.

'The cubicle is the matrix,' I said. 'This is the real world. Can we get down to business?'

Malini picked up a couple of paper napkins.

'As I said,' she said, 'I am a political science major. We face problems like this constantly, in international relations. I can analyze this.'

'Go ahead,' I said.

She drew a square on the napkin.

'This morning, you had Sathish. Aman and the rest were free.'

Another square.

'In the evening, Anderson had Sathish and Aman.'

Third square.

'Now, you have Sathish. Anderson has Aman. It is a classic zero-sum game situation. Anderson wants Sathish. He knows you will try to get Aman. Vice versa for you.'

'Yes, correct. What is the solution?'

'I cannot suggest a solution. I can only analyze,' she said.

'Thanks. Spoken like a liberal arts student,' said Raj.

'Wait,' she said. 'There is no solution for this current game. But you can change the game.'

'What do you mean?'

'You know that Anderson wants Sathish, for some reason. He, on the other hand, has no idea about your motivation. He does not know that you are a saintly, incorruptible person.'

'Uptight, humourless bastard,' said Raj.

'Yes. So that introduces an unknown in the game, which you can exploit.'

'I still do not understand,' I said.

'She means that you can call him and ask for money in exchange for Sathish.'

'Money? How much?'

Raj sighed. 'It does not matter. You ask for money, he comes to get Sathish and you follow him to locate Aman.'

'Yes,' said Malini. 'Right now, you do not know each others' location. You need to find his location. He needs to find yours.'

I had been engrossed in the discussion and not paying

attention to the rest of the restaurant. I suddenly realized that it seemed to have gone very quiet.

'I think you're wrong, Malini,' Raj said. 'He has already found us.'

I turned in my seat.

Two tall white guys were at the door, scanning the inside of the restaurant. Everyone was looking at them.

One of the white guys spotted us in the far corner. He nudged his companion and nodded in our direction. They started moving towards us.

'So much for game theory,' said Raj.

I waited. We had no time to run, not with Sathish.

The men stopped at our table. They smiled in unison.

'Care to go for a walk?' said the thinner one.

They looked at Sathish warily. I felt a twinge of pride. Our crazy CEO managed to inspire fear even while sleeping.

Raj slammed his glass of water on the table. 'No,' he said in a loud voice, getting up. By now, we had the attention of the whole restaurant.

'I don't think we are coming back to work,' he said.

The men looked confused.

'You don't have a choice,' the other white guy said.

'No, no way. We're exhausted. You can get out of here.'

I stared at him open-mouthed.

There was a small rumbling among the other patrons.

One of them sitting by our table got up and said, 'What is the problem?'

The white guys turned to look at him.

'You can sit down,' said the thinner one.

Raj threw up his hands. 'We are just tired of the deadlines, okay? It's a Friday and we are not going back.'

There were murmurs of sympathy from the crowd. A few people got up and started inching closer.

The white guys looked uneasy.

'Clients are not welcome here,' said the guy from the nearby table.

'Yeah, crawl back into your hole,' said someone.

The thinner white guy made the mistake of turning back and opening his jacket to show his gun.

'What the hell?' screamed a man in the back. 'They brought guns to force these guys.'

'I said clients are not welcome,' shouted our neighbour. The white guy put his hand in his jacket, for whatever reason. A table nearby shook and a chair flew straight at him. He caught it, full force, on his head and crashed down.

The other white man panicked and turned to run. Someone tackled him as he rushed for the door, and a few of the patrons jumped on him in a mess of dosa, sambhar and chutney.

The guy from the nearby table told us, 'Don't worry guys. They won't bother you again. Enjoy your weekend.'

Raj gently picked up Sathish and started walking out. Malini and I followed him. We skirted the mess in the middle where a very white man was having spicy chutney poured down his throat.

∞

The Honda was parked outside. We gave it a wide berth and got into our vehicle.

'Sir, can you proceed to Adyar?' Raj said to the driver.

'How did they get here?' whispered Malini.

'I was thinking about that,' Raj said. 'But, of course, they must have done this.' He opened Sathish's jacket and asked me to switch on the light. I did so and then leaned over from the front seat to take a look.

The lining was bulky. Something was stitched into the suit.

He traced his hand along the lining. There was a small zip. Undoing it, he brought out a small black object. It was square and filled his palm.

He raised it up and inspected it.

'GPS tracker,' he said.

'You sure? How do you know?'

'It says GPS tracker on it.'

'So they know our position now?'

'Yes. I suspected this when they walked in.'

'Can you turn it off?'

He was about to open it, when I stopped him.

'Actually, can we give it a false location? Make them go looking for us somewhere else?'

'Let's see. That would require us to reverse engineer its command sequence; figure out its receiver address; spoof the signal; but also send it along a path using a program so that the tracker does not suspect anything.'

'Yes, can you do it?'

'Are you kidding me? No. Certainly not any time soon.'

'Okay, switch it off.'

He opened the unit and pulled the batteries out.

'There. Now let's go to the expert,' he said.

He guided the driver to one of those fine streets in Adyar, tree-lined with neat rows of spectacular houses.

One of these houses had all sorts of antenna on its roof. We walked up to it, with Sathish in tow.

Raj rang the bell at the gate.

We could hear a dog bark wildly in the background. The door opened and a young man peeked out.

'Hi Raj,' he said.

'Need some help with a GPS unit,' Raj called out.

'Come on in.'

The young man looked curiously at Sathish as we trooped into the compound and onto the patio.

'Make yourselves comfortable,' he said.

Raj fished out the GPS tracking unit from his pocket and put it on the coffee table.

'We would like to know the receiver address,' he said.

The young man picked it up and inspected it.

'You have the batteries?'

Raj put the batteries on the table.

'You just need the receiver information?'

'Yes, how long will it take?'

The young man grimaced.

'Can you wait till tomorrow?'

'No, lives are at stake. We need it right now.'

He laughed. 'Lives are at stake? Really, Raj? Lives?'

'Believe me, this time.'

'Okay, I'll take a look. You had dinner yet?'

'Yes, thanks. We should go now. You'll call with the information?'

We got up.

'Where did you get this? Is your company using this to track you?'

'No, far more serious business.'

The young man laughed again and we left.

☙

'Where do we go now?' I said. 'We need a plan.'

We were still in Adyar, sitting in the car.

'I'm not sure finding the receiver address is going to help us,' said Raj. 'Particularly if they use a mobile network. The signal would go to some server that has nothing to do with Anderson.'

'So, back to square one – how do we find Anderson?'

'Maybe Aman had a way of contacting him.'

'Yes, but that is not much help now, is it?' I said.

'Well, we still have the EXM documents. They may have a clue,' said Raj.

'You mean a secret message?'

'Or something that we missed.'

He picked up his bag and opened his laptop. He had a data card, and accessed the internet.

'Here is their stupid vision statement,' he said.

Malini peered at it.

'Wow,' she said.

'Yes, pretty intense,' I said.

'What is this disclosure crap?' Raj asked.

I read the document again.

'It seems PH Capital may sue us for disclosing some of their details.'

'But,' Malini said, 'that means they are your company's clients.'

'Yes, it says former clients, right there.'

'Won't you have client contact details, such as their local address?' she said.

Raj and I looked at each other.

'That is actually confidential,' I said.

'Don't say it,' he said.

'Yes, Raj hacked into the Teams database just this

morning. We can find who worked with the PH Capital team.'

'You are a genius,' said Malini.

Raj was already typing furiously.

'I did hack into the database, but it is possible our local servers were all destroyed by sleeping beauty here,' he pointed at Sathish.

We sat in silence. The driver seemed to have no desire for food or sleep. He just stood outside, immobile.

'Okay, db is up,' said Raj. 'PH Capital, PH Capital . . .'

'Hey, why was there no big party for these people?' I asked.

Usually, when we had a new client, we got an excited announcement from the managers. They would bring in a client contact, from Europe or North America. The guy would get the royal treatment, and there would be cake-cutting and all that.

After some time, the project would end in a disaster or devolve into a bitter dispute at which point the client's name quietly disappeared from our website. Nobody ever spoke of them again, in polite company.

I did not remember any special announcement being made for PH Capital.

'They were called the Blaze team,' said Raj. 'I have it here. Client contact named Rupert. No phone, no address.'

'How did the team communicate with PH Capital?'

'We have to ask the team members. Hold on . . . The Blaze team at BSD had just two people. Subramanian and Samuel.'

'Do you know them?'

'Nope. I have their photographs here though.' He took a second and then said, 'No, don't recognize them. Can you check?'

I had very few friends at BSD. I certainly did not recognize these guys.

'Let me call them,' I said.

I took out the police cell phone and dialled as Raj called out Subramanian's phone number.

The phone kept ringing. After some time, I cut the call.

'Give me Samuel's number,' I said.

Samuel picked up on the second ring.

'Hi,' I said. 'Arjun Palani here. I work at BSD.'

'Oh, hi. How is everything there?'

I hesitated.

'You do not work at BSD anymore?'

'No. I had to leave back in September.'

'Did you work with the Blaze team?'

'Yes, why? Subbu wrote most of the code,' he said.

'Don't worry about the code. Who did you work with at PH Capital?'

'No one.'

'I don't understand.'

'I never dealt with the client. All issues went through Subbu.'

'Did you know this Rupert person?'

'Who? No.'

This was proving to be useless.

'Where is Subbu? Did he change his number?'

There was a pause at the other end.

'Who are you? Why do you need to contact Subbu?'

'My project manager asked me to contact PH Capital,' I lied.

'Oh, okay. Actually I do not know where Subbu is. I don't think *anyone* knows.'

I felt the hair standing up on my arms.

'What do you mean?'

'He went missing, back in September. They closed the project after that and I was asked to leave. The police kept asking me as well, but I really have no idea where he went.'

9

THE BLAZE WORM

We got Subbu's address from the employee database. 'Is it a good idea to go to his home so late?' Malini asked. It was ten o'clock, and his house was in Pallikaranai, on the way to the suburb of Tambaram. 'His parents may get upset.'

'We have no choice,' I said.

'The police have not found him after two months of searching, what is the point?' Malini asked.

'Let me explain,' I said. 'BSD had a team working with PH Capital. Suddenly, in September, just before all this started, Subbu, the lead programmer from that team, goes missing. Then the other programmer is laid off. Within a couple of weeks, Sathish here goes mad at the NASSCOM conference. Then the EXM team gets formed, I get pulled in, you get shot at and here we are, a few hours from a deadline to go fight a demon or whatever. What does this tell you?'

'It tells me that Subbu was made to disappear,' Raj said.

'Exactly. Maybe he is in the same location that Aman and the others are. Captive to Anderson. So, we have to find him,' I said.

'Malini, I think we should drop you home,' Raj said.

Suddenly, Sathish moaned. He slowly opened his eyes and sat up.

His eyes seemed clear.

He clutched his head and continued to sit still for some time, while we watched him warily.

'My head hurts,' he said.

Raj handed over a bottle of water. Sathish opened it and drank greedily.

Then he looked at us.

'Who are you? Where am I?' he said.

His eyes fell on Malini and his face softened.

'I remember you,' he said. 'You were in my dreams.'

'Hello Mr Sathish,' she said sweetly.

'I had horrible nightmares. I thought I was going to die,' he said.

We were turning onto the link road to Pallikaranai.

He bowed down and covered his face with his hands. His broad shoulders shook.

We remained silent as our CEO cried like a baby. Malini reached out and touched his shoulder. He flinched and then stopped shaking. Slowly he lay back on the seat and went to sleep again.

'Poor man,' said Malini.

'Maybe CEOs aren't bad people after all,' said Raj.

We sat in silence as the car bumped along a rough road. It was dark outside.

'Number 26,' the driver announced.

We got down from the car and looked up. It was a small, old apartment building. The address said the apartment was 2A.

We left Sathish in the car and trudged up to the second floor, dreading the encounter with the parents.

I rang the doorbell. The living room light was still on.

A man, probably in late fifties, opened the door. He looked at the three of us suspiciously.

'Yes?'

'We are from BSD Technologies. Subbu's colleagues,' said Malini.

'What? Why so late?'

'Sir,' continued Malini, 'we are on an urgent assignment. Your son may help us.'

'He is not here. We don't know where he is,' the man said.

From inside came a woman's voice, probably Subbu's mother. 'Who is it?' she asked.

The man opened the door wider and said, 'Come in.'

The living room was small. Neat. There was a photograph of Subbu in his graduation outfit on a wall.

The woman came out from the bedroom.

'Subbu's office people,' said the man, by way of introduction to her.

'Do you know where he is?' she asked.

'No, aunty,' Malini said. 'We are looking for some clues. We're trying to find him.'

'But the police have been trying for two months,' said the man.

'Who was the inspector, Sir?' asked Raj.

'Someone named Vishal. He was from Crime Branch.'

'Yes, Sir. We know him,' Raj said.

They seemed to get a little more confident hearing that.

'He left for work as usual, on September 16. They say he never reached BSD. No one has seen him. Are they telling the truth? Is it some issue at work?' the woman asked.

'It seems there could be a bigger issue, aunty,' Malini said. 'We do not know right now.'

'We tried to speak to the CEO. We always felt he was hiding something,' Subbu's father said.

'Then he went crazy,' the woman added.

'Aunty, can we look at his room?' Raj asked.

'Yes, but the police have been there,' she said. She opened a door to the left. 'This was his room.'

We walked past her into the room. The bed was in a corner. One wall was taken up by a poster from the film *The Matrix*. It was of Neo, facing off against Mr Smith.

The other walls had bookshelves. Raj walked over and checked them.

'The police took his computer,' said Subbu's mother, who had followed us in.

I looked at the books. They were all technical – PHP, C, Assembly programming books.

Raj seemed to be looking for something. He was opening each book methodically.

'Did he spend a lot of time in this room, aunty?' he asked.

'Yes, always in front of his computer.'

Finally Raj picked up a book and called Malini and me over.

On the back cover, there was a drawing. It was a drawing of a mask.

'Do you know this?' he said.

'I saw this recently in the newspapers,' Malini said.

'It is a Guy Fawkes mask.'

Raj turned to the woman and said, 'Thank you, aunty.' We walked out of the room. Subbu's father was watching television.

'Thanks, uncle,' Malini said.

'Can you find him?' Subbu's mother asked.

'I think we are closer, aunty,' Raj said.

As we were about to leave, Raj turned and said, 'Did you call him by some other name, some pet name, at home?'

The woman smiled. 'Yes. We called him Chikku. It means little boy in Kannada.'

༚

'What does that mask indicate?' I asked Raj, on the way down.

'You may have seen the mask when they protested the Internet censorship bills, a year back. It is a symbol for the hackers group, Anonymous.'

'I've heard of Anonymous, but are they in India?' said Malini.

'Yes, they have an offshoot here – and it is likely they have people in Chennai.'

We reached the car and piled in.

'Where to now?' I asked.

'Let us think a little bit. First, I need a good internet connection. I think we will be better off closer to the IT Corridor,' Raj said.

The car slowly pulled out. We drove along the marshlands of Pallikaranai. The road cut through this famous marsh, refuge for thousands of migratory birds until the Chennai city corporation decided to locate its garbage dump yard right there. In addition to which they also burnt the garbage. Sweet corporation. The birds were now getting the hell out of Pallikaranai. If I were them, I would skip Chennai altogether.

'You done with your thinking?' Malini asked.

'I'm just not sure what to do next. I looked at his books. He is obviously a very smart guy. And he is an expert in

C and Assembly. I found the book *Ethical Hacking*; along with the mask symbol, it is very likely he is a member of Anonymous.'

'You think they got rid of him because of that?'

'What? No. The government thinks Anonymous India is a joke. And he may yet be alive. He could have left his home voluntarily.'

I said, with impatience, 'Sure, but isn't it more probable that he is in trouble with PH Capital?'

'Yes,' Raj conceded.

'What does this Anonymous thing mean for us?'

'They could know more about him. It is possible he let them know what was going on.'

'Okay, who do we contact in Anonymous? How can you even possibly contact an underground group?'

Raj was silent.

I turned to look at him.

'Wait a minute,' said Malini.

'Yes,' Raj said.

'*You* are a member of Anonymous?'

Raj did not say anything.

'But that is so cool!'

'I am neither confirming nor denying your statement,' he said.

'So, you should be able to find out if Subbu contacted you guys?'

'You don't understand. For that I need Subbu's online identity. But, also, it is not a close-knit group. There is no real leader. There is no central information.'

'But this is so cool,' repeated Malini.

'I am a member of our apartment association,' I informed her.

She ignored me.

We stopped the car near the toll gate. Raj hunched over his computer.

His phone rang.

'Yes?' he said. Then he looked at us and said, 'It is Akram.'

'Who?'

'GPS expert.'

'I am putting you on speaker phone,' he said, into the phone.

'Hey, you all,' said Akram's tinny voice.

'Could you find the receiver address?'

'Well,' said Akram. 'There is a small issue.'

'What is it?'

'First, the tracker is not using GPRS. I think they wanted more coverage and did not want to depend on mobile networks. Which is strange. So, the good news is they are communicating directly with their own receiver.'

'Okay, where is the receiver?'

'That is the problem. First they have a small battery pack. They are using low power transmission. The whole thing would go out of range within one or two kilometres.'

Raj thought about this.

'So, the GPS tracker was transmitting signals within a short distance? What is the point of that?'

'I don't know. So it is not a very effective tracker, unless the receiver is close by.'

'But,' said Raj, 'we went from one corner of the city to another today, and they could still trace us.'

'Yes, okay.'

'What does that mean?'

'I don't know. Maybe they have multiple receivers like a mobile network across the city.'

'That does not make any sense.'

'Yes.'

Raj looked thoughtful.

'All right, I may need your help later tonight.'

'No problem. I exist to serve you on Friday nights.'

Akram hung up.

'This guy is from Anonymous too?' asked Malini.

'No idea,' said Raj. 'Could be. The smart people usually are.'

Malini gave me a pitying look.

∾

Raj sat back.

'One way to find out more about the Blaze team is to look for Subbu's online account. It is usually difficult to track,' he said, 'but we know some details about him. We think he is a member of Anonymous, and that he worked with PLCs and machine interfaces. We can do a cross-search. There are a couple of website forums. I could start with 4chan.'

'There were books on PLCs in his room,' I said.

'Yes. It is unusual for our company to work with PLCs.'

'What are PLCs?' Malini asked.

'Programmable Logic Controllers. They are machine interfaces. Most Indian IT service companies do not work with them.'

'I could look in the Indian forums for PLC postings,' Raj said.

I got down and went over to the back to sit next to him.

'I see someone called Chik24 who posted in PLC forums a few months back,' he said.

'This seems a bit roundabout. Can't you simply look in

Anonymous India forums and check if some active member is missing?'

Raj stopped typing and looked at me.

'Most members are not active,' he said. 'But, it is possible that the PLC forum guy used the same identity in 4chan. I need some custom script to check that.'

He started typing in the script.

My walkie-talkie buzzed.

I picked it up and looked at it. It said 'Aman' on the display.

I pushed the Connect button.

'Hi Arjun,' said Anderson's voice.

'Hi.'

'I will admit,' he said, 'you have surprised me.'

I was silent.

'I'm curious, do you know why you were recruited?'

Raj and Malini were looking at me.

'What is your point, Mr Anderson?' I said.

'If you knew what was going to happen to you tonight, maybe we could come to an agreement.'

'I'm listening.'

'Your bosses are not as virtuous as you think.'

'As bosses go?' I said.

He laughed.

'I would like you to hand Sathish over. We have some unfinished business with him.'

Raj grabbed the walkie-talkie from me and turned it over. He looked at the model number and mouthed 'Cut' to me, as he drew his hand across his neck.

I hesitated. Then pushed the button to cut the call.

'It's a Nextar model,' Raj said. 'They can trace you when you talk.'

'Should we leave?'

'Yes, although they did not have enough time to triangulate you.'

His computer pinged.

'One match' blinked the console.

'Okay, we have a match between the PLC forum and 4chan. Let's see,' said Raj.

The computer showed the matching search expression.

'Entry is from early September. That fits with our timeline,' he said.

The web link showed us the post snippet.

Siemens 7050H seems to have a bug — where would I get the full command definition? said the post by Neo120282.

Numerous posts with 'Neo120282' popped up in 4chan. The last one was on September 17. Raj clicked on the link.

The post was not by Neo, but it mentioned Neo120282 in the content.

Vdo pkg frm Neo120282. Ne1 know hw to dec it?

'What does that mean?' said Malini.

'I think the poster got a video file from Neo and did not know how to decode it.'

I checked on the left for the id of the person who had posted it. It said ElfLegolas.

'You think Neo was Subbu's online name?'

'Could be. Worth pursuing,' said Raj.

We watched as Raj opened his secure chat program. He chose a contact named Melvin.

'You there?'

''sup?'

'You know anything about ElfLegolas in 4chan?'

There was a brief pause.

'Yes. Why?'

'Can you ask him to contact me? Like right now? It's about a video he received.'

'Legolas is a busy man. But I'll pass on your message.'

∾

Malini's mother called. She seemed to have woken up to the fact that her only child was missing, at around eleven o'clock at night.

'Yes, Amma,' said Malini.

She listened.

'Who? When did they come? . . . I am with the police. We are trying to help this crazy man. No, I won't go home. Don't worry.'

She hung up.

'It seems there have been a couple more visits by Anderson's people to my house,' she said.

'Is your mother safe?'

'She's fine. Just irritated. She wants to bring people from her home town to kill these guys.'

We laughed at that. Cute family.

'So,' she said. 'What is this Subbu guy doing with PLCs? Why would PH Capital try to get him?'

We looked through Neo's postings for some time. In the PLC forums, they were mostly about a Siemens controller.

'Siemens 7050H,' said Raj. 'Used in compressors for cooling. Subbu was working with that.'

'Maybe this was something he did on the side,' I said.

'We can find out. BSD's internal portal has all source code checked in automatically,' said Raj.

He was logging into the BSD servers again.

'Why would a hedge fund company work with compressors and other hardware?' I said.

'Maybe their air-conditioning sucked,' Malini grinned.

Raj's Skype window buzzed. It was a new contact – Legolas.

'Hi,' Raj typed.

'Can we talk?' came the reply from Legolas.

'Yes. I have two of my colleagues here with me.'

The little phone on the Skype window started buzzing. Raj picked up the call.

'Hi, it's Legolas here.'

'Hi,' said Raj.

'You were asking about a video I received? Why are you interested in that?'

'I think I know the identity of Neo. We think he is a colleague and he has been missing for the past two months.'

'Yes. We have missed him too,' Legolas said.

There was a brief silence.

'I have heard of you,' said Legolas. 'I have heard good things about you. Let me explain what we are facing. Maybe you can help us.'

Legolas was a slow talker who enunciated each word clearly, as people who dealt with multiple cultures are wont to do.

'Three months back,' he said, 'I was approached through our network by this man, Neo120282. He did not reveal his real identity. He said he worked with a software services company in Chennai.

'Neo had been working on a project for some financial sector client from the United States. The project was unusual for his employer. It dealt with PLCs. Specifically, he was required to issue a few commands to a Siemens PLC interface. The coding itself was not complex, but Neo thought he was not being given the complete picture.

His client contact was very secretive. And once the core coding was done, they disappeared, while Neo was asked to sit around doing nothing. From time to time, he was asked to change a few lines of code.

'Neo began to suspect that his client was actually working with another vendor, another team. He did not know where this team was. But they were using his compiled code. They did not know he existed. He finally discovered them by accident, through a careless email.

'Neo dug further, as any of us would. It was at this point that he first contacted us, Anonymous India. He communicated a message to me, while I was busy with the protests. He said he had evidence of a major plot to influence global markets.

'Initially we thought he was a crackpot. End of August, Neo seemed desperate. He said he had contacted his CEO with details of the plot. In order to prove his credentials, he made a prediction to us. We still ignored him.

'As you know, in mid-September, I received a video from his account. I do not know what to make of this video. It's horrible. I hope it's doctored. But all communication with Neo stopped from that day.'

'What is in the video?' asked Raj.

'I'm sending it to you,' Legolas said.

The Skype window pinged. He was transferring a file.

Raj started saving it.

I said, 'Mr Legolas, this is Arjun. You said you thought Neo was a crackpot. What made you change your mind?'

'As I said, he made a prediction. It came true a few weeks back. It made me realize that it was a mistake to ignore him.'

'What did he predict?'

The Skype window pinged with a message. It was a web link from Legolas. Raj clicked on it.

A browser window opened with a BBC Online article. *Refinery fire in Saudi Arabia*, said the headline.

The article was about a fire in a small crude oil refinery near Jeddah. The fire had been put down fast. No casualties and almost no downtime.

'Neo predicted a fire?' I asked.

'He predicted a fire in Saudi Arabia, in this refinery. He said it would happen within a month and that this was a test run – for a much bigger cyber attack.'

'A cyber attack?' I laughed. 'How can you cyber attack a refinery?'

'Have you heard of Stuxnet, Arjun?' Legolas asked.

'What is that?'

Raj answered instead. 'It's a computer worm that was used to attack the Natanz nuclear reactor in Iran, three years back. Computer worms are already used to attack hardware interfaces.'

'Hold on,' I said. 'You're saying that Neo wrote the program that caused this refinery fire?'

'It seems likely,' said Legolas.

10

THE EYE IN THE SKY

Raj played the video from Legolas.

An image of the ocean came up. The angle was from the top. Waves were breaking on a rectangular structure.

Then the camera moved and zoomed in.

The rectangular structure was a pier. There was a black object on it.

As the camera zoomed in further, we could see that the object was a man. Lying face down. He was twitching.

Then he slowly turned over. The camera zoomed in on his face.

The image was grainy. We peered closely.

Then a shadow hid the man's face. A huge shadow.

A big man stepped in with his back to the camera. His legs were on either side of the man on the pier.

The big man bent down, and slowly sat down on the defenceless man.

The dark man seemed to be screaming. There was no sound on the video.

The big man put his enormous hands on either side of his neck and started squeezing.

'Oh my god,' Malini murmured.

The three-minute video slowly played out as the man

lying down was strangled. Malini turned away.

The video stopped with some text on a dark screen:

Anon – get the message

'Oh my god, what is this?' Malini said.

'Can you play it again?' I asked. 'I recognize the big man.'

Raj played the video again.

'It's Big Bruce. The man who attacked you today,' I said to Malini.

'Who was it that he killed?'

'We can guess, can't we?' said Raj.

'You think it is Subbu?'

'Yes. Undoubtedly. They killed him and wanted to send a message to Anonymous in case someone decided to interfere. He must have been killed on the day he went missing.'

I felt tears in my eyes. His parents were waiting for him still, at home. Thinking he would return.

How were we going to tell them?

Till now, this had been a game of cat and mouse, but I felt cold fury at these men. What had Subbu done to deserve this?

'We should hand this over to the police,' Malini said.

Raj stayed silent.

I shook my head. 'We still have to complete what we set out to do.'

'What? Play around with GPS and all that? Let us just go and bring the police in.'

I glanced at the driver standing outside.

'Listen, Vishal, the inspector, is in touch with this Anderson guy. I do not think the police will help us now.'

'We have to continue what we are doing,' Raj said.

'Yes. First, Raj, who filmed this video?' I said.

'I noticed that too. Unusual angle.'

'Was it from a building close to the pier?'

We played the video again.

'You notice in the first few seconds that the camera is looking straight down at the ocean?' I said.

'Yes. Then it moves to the pier.'

'Is it a helicopter? Someone filming this from a helicopter?'

'Could be,' said Raj. 'But I think there is something else going on.'

He picked up his phone and called Akram.

'Hi, I was waiting for your call,' Akram said.

'Listen, man, you are on speaker phone. You mentioned that they may have a network of receivers, right?'

'Yes, otherwise the GPS tracker is not very useful.'

'Could it be that the receiver is also mobile, moving around?'

'Along with the tracker? What is the point of that?'

'Bear with me. Is it possible that it's actually a single mobile receiver?'

'Sure, yes.'

'Could it be in the air?'

'Like a helicopter that keeps running around a GPS tracker? I expected more from you, Raj. First, you would have heard the helicopter.'

'Not a helicopter. A drone,' said Raj.

There was silence from the other end. Then we heard a low whistle.

'Are you kidding me? Really? A drone in Chennai?'

'Well, it explains something else we found just now.'

'Boy, it would be very nice if I could get my hands on

one. You really think there is a drone flying around our airspace?'

'Yes, and I want you to triangulate its base station. Can you come over with your magic equipment to the toll booth on IT Corridor?'

'Dude, I am on my way.'

He hung up.

'Can you explain?' Malini said.

'You must know what drones are,' Raj said. He looked at our blank faces. 'Surely you have heard of the bombing campaigns in Pakistan by a secret American program?'

'Secret to Americans. Not to Pakistanis,' Malini said.

'Yes, yes, so they are using these remote-operated, unmanned aerial vehicles. They are called UAVs or drones. Small, undetectable on radar.'

'But I thought only the US government had access to them,' said Malini. 'Are we fighting those guys?'

'No, drones are actually meant for industrial usage. They are also cheap. It is likely that PH Capital has access to them.'

'More and more, they do not seem like a financial company to me,' I said. 'Sounds like the mafia.'

'But why do you think there is a drone up there?' Malini asked.

'Two reasons. The camera shot we saw is clearly from an aerial vehicle. Secondly, the GPS tracker was working with a mobile receiver. It was sending its signal to a receiver close by. That receiver must, then, be sending them to Anderson's team. It is likely that the receiver is in the air,' he said.

'We are going to take the drone out?' I asked.

'No. Akram can get the drone by feeding false GPS

coordinates. But, in our case, we do not need the drone. We need to know where its communication goes. Someone is operating it remotely, from Chennai. And maybe that is where Anderson has his base.'

∾

We called Legolas and informed him about the drone.

'Interesting,' he said. 'You are making a lot of progress.'

He was silent for a few seconds.

Then he said, 'You guys should understand, we are not used to offline action, other than protests. I don't know what Neo thought we could do. I was not prepared to handle this kind of a mega-plot by a multinational corporation.'

'I don't think you should blame yourself for not believing Neo,' Raj said.

'Yes, except that he is now dead.'

'We still do not know that for sure.'

He was silent again.

'You guys are now in a unique position,' he said. 'You know Neo's offline identity. You probably even have access to his code. If you identify the other part of the puzzle, we could actually try to move against these PH Capital guys.'

'What would you like us to do?' I asked.

'All that Neo handled was the communication with the PLC and some other interfaces. If this program, Blaze, is built like the Stuxnet worm, someone must have built the rest of it. Neo thought there was another team, probably also in India. If we find the rest of the code, we can probably stop this program from doing too much damage.

'I should also tell you,' Legolas continued, 'Neo was frustrated with our disbelief and inaction. Towards the end, he said he was going to contact his CEO to help reveal the plot to the public.'

Legolas signed off, after promising that we could reach him anytime through the night.

❧

'I remember Stuxnet,' said Malini. 'There was another virus, I think, called the Flame. They were part of the attempt to shut down Iran's reactors.'

'So, PH Capital is having Indian programmers write something that will take down Saudi oil refineries? Why?' said Raj.

'Let's trace this from the beginning. One thread is that PH Capital, for some reason, wants to shut down oil refineries. They work with two teams to hide the true nature of the program. One of the programmers figures out what they are doing. He is then eliminated.'

'Right. And Sathish is in trouble because Subbu spoke to him about the plot,' Raj said.

'Exactly. But I'm not sure where this exorcism comes in. You think Aman and his team know about all these details?'

'You know, to hell with Aman,' said Raj. 'He could have clearly laid out what he knew and what he did not. Instead here we are, trying to figure out everything by ourselves.'

'It is a leadership quality,' I said. 'MBA is mostly about teaching managers how to hide information.'

It was midnight when Akram finally made it. I had, by then, received frantic calls from Idumban.

'Can you go?' Idumban had asked me.

'Where?'

'To Ahi? I can explain the whole process to you.'

'Thanks. I am but a small cog in this giant machine. It is only proper that I wait for my superiors.'

He laughed.

'Get them here as soon as you can,' he said.

∽

Akram came in a big Pajero SUV. It had a small transmitter antenna on top.

'Let's go drone catching,' he said happily.

We told the driver he could leave and thanked him. It did not make sense to have a policeman with us while we snooped around private property.

The SUV's rear was a small working space, with a laptop and a few gadgets. Akram sat in the middle of it. We put Sathish in the front passenger seat, and crowded around Akram in the back.

'The tracker is at four thirteen megahertz,' he said. 'The drone could be receiving signals at any range, but is likely to be in that same frequency. We can scan frequencies. But, here is the first step.'

He put the batteries back in the GPS tracker.

'Now, let's look for the drone,' he said.

'The frequency scanner looks for a pattern in a loop,' he explained as we waited.

Nothing happened in the first scan.

'Let's start driving around. Raj, can you drive?'

'Where to?'

'We have to go diagonally from east to west,' Akram said.

'Can I suggest something?' I said.

'Yes?'

'We know a guy, an inspector, who can be tapped for this. I can call him and tell him where we are. The information is sure to reach our adversaries, and the drone will be sent over.'

'Oh, you have adversaries . . . interesting. I thought you were doing this for one of your juvenile games, Raj. Okay, call this inspector. Let's use him as bait to get the drone.'

I had Vishal's number saved in the phone he had given me. I dialled, hoping he had recovered by now.

He seemed to be up and about. 'Hello?' he said.

'Hello, Sir. This is Arjun. From BSD.'

There was a pause.

'Where are you, Arjun?'

I thought about how to answer this. Anderson may have conveyed to Vishal that we had Sathish and were running around town dodging him. It was best to work on that assumption.

'Sir, we have the CEO, Sathish Kumar. We have had a few problems. But we are planning to go back to the IG office to check some information.'

'Okay . . .'

'How are you, Sir? Is everything all right?'

'Yes, I had a concussion. They may not allow you into the office so late,' he said.

'That is why we are calling you. Can you tell them to let us in?'

Vishal seemed to hesitate. Then he made up his mind and said, 'You guys can go over there. Wait at the gate and I will tell someone to come over.'

He hung up.

'Okay, let's head that side but stay clear of the IG office. The drone should arrive in that neighbourhood,' I said.

We started driving towards the IG office, northward, close to the beach. It was five or six kilometres away. There was no traffic at this time of the night.

Akram kept tracking. Suddenly we heard a small pinging sound from the laptop.

'This could be it,' he said.

Raj stopped the car in a corner.

'Unplug the tracker,' Akram said.

I fiddled with the GPS tracker and unplugged the battery. The pings stopped.

'What is going on?' Malini asked.

'The remote operator has noted that the signal disappeared. He's uncertain,' Akram explained.

He typed a command on the laptop.

'Let's move the car,' he said.

Raj started the car again and we drove in complete silence.

'Plug in the batteries,' Akram said.

I put in the batteries. After a few seconds the pings resumed.

We all stared at the screen. Raj had stopped the car.

Akram waited and then said, 'Unplug again.'

I pulled out the batteries.

Akram pressed a button and a map opened up on the laptop. He pointed and said, 'Here is the drone.'

The map had a superimposed GPS coordinate. I peered at it.

'It is right above us,' Akram said.

Malini moved to open the window.

'Don't,' he said. 'You can't see it anyway. And it can probably see you.'

The pings resumed and the map refreshed.

'It's moving away,' he said.

'But why do we need the drone's location?' I asked. 'We need the location of the base station.'

'Patience. I have that too,' he said. 'But first, let's discuss some terms. Raj. The drone is mine.'

'Who cares? Take the freaking thing, if you can.'

'Okay. And I would like to be paid for further work.'

'I pointed you to the most valuable technology of current times, right over Chennai, you ingrate.'

'Yes, which is why I am not charging you now. You have to pay an hourly rate from tomorrow.'

Raj pointed at Malini. 'Her grandfather is a demon. I could send him after you.'

'Forty dollars an hour.'

'Please just tell us the damn location,' I said.

'All in good time. Raj, turn the car.'

We started going back the way we'd come.

'It is past the toll booth,' Akram said.

'What's the plan when we get there?' Raj asked.

'I'll go after the drone,' Akram said.

'Not you. Arjun, how do we get into this place?'

Akram chuckled as he looked at his laptop.

'What?'

'You're going to have some fun getting in here.'

Raj continued to drive.

I thought for some time.

'Can we have the drone launch a diversion? Like crash into this place?' Malini asked.

'Hey. That's not fair!' Akram grumbled.

'Hold on,' said Raj. 'That's a good idea. Akram, can you rig up a transmitter that will spoof GPS coordinates and instruct the drone to land?'

'Ya, sure. It's been done before. But let's not crash the drone.'

'We'll see.'

We passed the toll booth.

'Where now?'

'Keep driving,' Akram said.

My walkie-talkie buzzed. I glanced at the display.

'Anderson is trying to contact me again.'

'Don't connect the call. Let him keep guessing where we are.'

My cell phone started ringing. It was Vishal.

'Don't pick up.'

We went past the BSD offices, the Sholinganallur crossing and were now headed for Siruseri, further south.

'You may want to slow down,' Akram said.

'Can you please tell us the location already?'

'Slow down. Now switch off your lights,' Akram said, ignoring me.

We drove past a hotel.

'There, to your left. Stop here,' he said.

Raj pulled over to the shoulder and stopped. It was dark; the time was one o'clock in the morning.

We stared at the big building, bathed in light, a little bit ahead.

'But this is WTIC,' said Raj.

'Yes, that is where the drone is being controlled from,' Akram said.

11

IN YOUR BASE AND KILLING YOUR DOODZ

WTIC Systems: Indian IT companies as General Motors: American car companies.

One of the employers that programmers hated. Bureaucratic; slow; worked with Microsoft. It was one of the big five IT outsourcing giants, building its reputation on being really slow. Slow translated to security, respectability and predictability for clients.

'This does not make any sense. Why would Anderson be here?' I asked Raj.

'Arjun,' said Raj. He had a big smile on his face.

'We have found the other vendor, the other team that programmed Blaze.'

'You mean Anderson is sitting with the programmers in this building?'

'Probably. Makes sense to me. WTIC probably has a certification process for pier-side murders.'

Akram cleared his throat.

'Can I now go and get my drone?'

'Stay here and wait for our signal,' Raj said.

We got out and stood in the dark, staring at the huge software development centre.

'You know,' I said, 'I have spent all my life trying to sneak out of offices. I have no clue how to sneak *into* one. How do we get in there?'

'It's a problem,' agreed Raj. 'But we need to get in and find where Anderson is sitting.'

A steady stream of people was walking in and out of the building. A bunch of them were heading towards a nearby teashop.

'Maybe we should have Malini try her feminine charms with those guys?' I said.

Raj and Malini glared at me.

'Sorry . . .'

Raj dialled ElfLegolas.

'WTIC?' Legolas said after we'd updated him. 'Let me see if Anonymous has someone in there. Can you stay put for half an hour?'

'Sure,' said Raj and hung up.

'Now what do we do?' Malini asked.

'We try to look at the Blaze source code,' said Raj.

All the source code of BSD's programs was available in a central repository. This server was called a 'source control system', because it could keep different versions of the code. This gave a map of how the coding evolved as the program was being built. Some technical person at BSD had decided this should be opened up to everyone. We were all meant to look at each other's code and 'improve'. In practice, though, this meant our coding was a public source of embarrassment. People pointed and laughed in the cafeteria – that was the net result.

Raj had access to the source control system; he had already downloaded the latest version of Blaze. He was now looking through its history.

'Hmm . . . Someone has deleted newer versions of the code.'

'Who?'

He took some time before he looked up.

'Says here Subbu deleted his own code from the system, starting in August.'

'Why would he do that?'

'I've been thinking about this,' he said. 'Let's say you're a smart programmer, like me. If I'm asked to build something that is unethical, as part of my job, you know what I would do?'

'Resign in protest?' Malini asked.

'No, that would tell them I'm on to their game. And the program would continue by other means. What I would do is to put an Easter egg in the code.'

'You mean, put in a secret bug?' I said.

'Correct. The code would work in testing, but will fail when in a harmful system. Also, the programmers of Stuxnet themselves had put in ways for the worm to destroy itself. It checked to see if some remote server was accessible and looked for a specific file. If the file was found, it destroyed itself.'

'You think Subbu put in secret code and then handed over that version to PH Capital?'

'Yes, and made sure no one could find it. He must have destroyed the versions in source control.'

This is a nightmare, I thought. That meant the source code version did not match the running version. Nobody could fix such a program, now that Subbu was dead.

'There are ways to figure out what he did,' said Raj. 'There are disassemblers. We'll see what we can do.'

Legolas called back in ten minutes.

'Okay, I found someone who knows someone. You now have our full support to take these guys down,' he said.

'I'm happy to know that. I'll let you know my bank information.'

Legolas laughed.

'We're sending a guy named DarkKnight over. He says he works in WTIC and can probably take you into the building.'

He was about to hang up when Raj said, 'Hold on. Did you get any other communication from Neo in August?'

'Communication such as?'

'Archive files?'

'No.'

∾

DarkKnight arrived shortly. He was a tall, fair guy. He refused to give us his real name, although his ID badge was hanging from around his neck, right in front of us.

'Call me Knight,' he said mysteriously. 'Are you on Operation Neo?'

We had no idea whether or not that was the name that had been given, but we nodded eagerly.

'Are you all sworn?' he demanded.

'Sworn to what?'

He shook his head, as if disappointed with us, and started mumbling under his breath.

'Okay, let's plan this operation,' he said.

'How do we get in without swipe cards?' asked Raj.

'We are tunnelling under the electrified fence,' he said.

We looked at him in shock.

'Are you kidding?'

'Yes, of course I'm kidding. One of you can go in using my ID,' he said.

'What is the layout inside?' asked Raj, as if he were a professional thief.

'There are two big buildings and one small one within the complex. There is also a golf course,' explained Knight. 'We play cricket there, unless clients are visiting.'

'Do you have clients visiting now?' asked Raj.

'You mean, are there white guys on campus?' Knight said and laughed at his own joke.

'Yes.'

'You see that building?' he pointed at the smaller building on the left, a little way off. 'There are a few teams there. One of those teams is now doing a release. They have clients over.'

'A big guy among them?'

'Yes. I saw a huge white man. What's your plan?' Knight asked.

'We need to get into the building with the white guys,' Raj said.

'You can't. It has a separate access card.'

'What do you suggest?'

'You could climb up the drain pipes.'

We looked at each other.

'No, is there any other route we can take?'

He mulled over this.

'A couple of days back they sent an SOS from one of those teams,' he said.

'What's an SOS?'

'In theory it means that the services of the company's smart people are required by a particular team. In practice, it means we all stay the hell away from any team that sends an SOS.'

'So, one of those teams is having trouble?'

'Yes, and the clients may not know they are in trouble. The company usually informs the clients last, when a problem breaks out.'

Raj thought about this.

'Maybe you can volunteer your services,' he said.

'No, I need to stay undercover, thanks,' Knight replied.

'You can probably volunteer,' Malini said, to Raj.

'I'm not even from this company. They will be suspicious,' Raj said.

'First of all,' said Knight, 'just volunteering for an SOS will make them suspicious. I have not heard of any sane person volunteering to work on another team's problems in my life. Second, they will find out quickly, when you cannot solve their problem.'

'Oh, he can solve any problem,' Malini said.

I ground my teeth. I needed to brush up on my technical skills – apparently times had changed, and now, it seemed, women actually dug geeks.

Raj thought about Malini's suggestion for some time.

'Our other alternative is to crash the drone into that building and create a diversion,' Malini said.

Knight looked at her in puzzlement.

'Crash what?'

'Never mind. Let's try this,' said Raj. 'Let me first volunteer, try to get in and get you people in. If I'm caught, we can crash the drone.'

'What is this drone business?' Knight said.

'Nothing,' we all said in chorus.

The secret knowledge of mysterious plots was like a drug high for me. Maybe this was how executives felt every day.

'Who do I go and talk to?' asked Raj.

Knight gestured towards Raj's laptop bag.

'Can you open your computer? Let me show you the email.'

༄

SOS from Team Blaze, said the email subject.

Are you looking for a challenging problem that tests the limits of your brainpower?

We request assembly language experts or people experienced with disassemblers and PLCs to volunteer help solve a crucial, Level 4 issue for the Blaze team.

All volunteers will be rewarded with a signed certificate from our clients.

Interested, please call Jagan at extension 4214.

'Signed certificates?' Malini said.

'I know,' said Knight. 'Very exciting.'

'It says the Blaze team. They have the same name as Subbu's team,' she said.

'Yes, they are the ones having problems. Which fits in with what we discussed about the source code. It's obvious that they are not able to operate the Blaze program correctly,' Raj said.

'Let's call Jagan,' I said.

'First, let's get our backup plan ready,' said Raj. 'Arjun, I'll text you Akram's phone number. When he gets a message from us he'll feed in false landing data to the drone.' He started sending the contact.

'Why are you going alone?' Malini said. 'All of us can volunteer.'

We looked at her with pity.

'An engineer volunteering to fix another team's issue is unusual,' said Raj. 'Probably the last time it happened was in the Stone Age. Three of us together would warp the space-time continuum and explode the universe.'

∾

As directed by Knight, Raj called the switchboard number and was directed to Jagan's extension. Almost immediately, Jagan picked up.

'This is Raj. I'd like to volunteer for your PLC issue,' he said into the phone.

There was a pause.

'No, I am not smoking pot,' Raj said.

Another pause.

'I'm free right now. Can I come over? . . . Okay. I forgot my access card. Can you swipe me in? . . . Great, thanks.'

He hung up.

'Guy was shocked. Anyway, I can go over there right now. They're all working day and night apparently.'

'What should we do?'

'Stay here. I will go in first and then find some way to get you in.'

'Be careful,' Malini said.

∾

Akram kept looking at his laptop screen. Sathish was still out cold. Malini seemed lost in her thoughts or was sleepy.

'Akram, you know anything about Stuxnet?' I asked.

He looked up reluctantly.

'Yes, the worm that affected Iranian nuclear reactors.'

'How did they detect it?'

He warmed up.

'First, Stuxnet was only supposed to affect a single nuclear reactor,' he said. 'It was supposed to be dormant in any other system. Should not have been detected at all.'

'What happened?'

'I don't know. Probably some bug. It spread to many systems in Iran, India and Israel. They detected it because it was causing a computer to go on an infinite reboot cycle in Iran. Symantec's engineers spent a lot of time disassembling it.'

'But,' I said, 'how did it spread beyond its original target?'

'Yes. Good question. I assume you have written programs for computers?'

I was offended.

'Yes, of course.'

'Then you must be familiar with the esoteric concept of bugs, flaws in code?'

'You mean there were bugs that caused Stuxnet to spread and affect other systems?'

'Yes, I guess so.'

I thought about this.

'This means that the new virus they are coding could also have spread?'

'I gathered that you are trying to stop a Stuxnet-like virus,' Akram said. 'Yes, it could; but do you know if it was even released outside its test environment?'

'That is what this guy from Anonymous told us,' I said excitedly. 'He said there was a small refinery fire that was contained quickly, in Saudi Arabia. That must have meant a release outside, right?'

'Could be. If it was released for testing purposes, it is possible that the virus stayed there. Or it could have spread. Very likely that it spread.'

'And if you are a programmer wishing to draw attention to the virus, you probably want it to spread, and catch the attention of Symantec and other anti-virus guys.'

'Yes.'

I thought about this some more.

'Can I have your computer? I need to look up something,' I said.

He handed over his laptop. I started keying in a few searches.

The Knight was staring at Sathish, laid out on the front seat.

'Is that who I think it is?' he asked suddenly.

I looked up. 'Yes,' I said.

He was silent for some time. Then he said, 'He was here, you know.'

'Really, when was that?' I asked, continuing to work on the laptop.

'A couple of months back, I think. When they set up the lab in the cemetery, over there,' he gestured to a corner of the grounds.

I sat up.

'Cemetery? Lab? What do you mean?'

'This building is new,' he said. 'It is built right on top of an old burial ground. We joke about it all the time. You see there, at the back?' he said.

I peered at the WTIC buildings.

'Where?'

'Behind the small building, you see where it is dark? They left a portion of the cemetery standing and built a set of rooms there. We call it the Cemetery lab. This guy was there.'

I looked at Malini. She seemed horrified too.

'Why do you call it the lab?' she said.

'They have a set of weird guys there, and some ancient pots and pans. Nobody goes there at night. We can hear screaming, and you know the udukku?' he asked.

The udukku was a small instrument that, in spite of its size, managed to raise the creepiest rhythmic sound in the world. We all knew about it, of course. It was used by the guys who hung around crematoriums. The deity Shiva held it in his hand while dancing around with his consort Sati's dead body.

'Yes, we know the udukku,' I said.

'You can hear that sound, even from the cafeteria, on quiet nights.'

I shuddered.

Knight continued. 'A few days after we saw him, he went nuts. We all thought he saw something in the lab. I hope nothing happens to the other guys.'

'Other guys?'

'Yes, this guy is from BSD, no? The top management from BSD was there, at the lab today. I saw them drive in.'

'Wait a minute,' I said. 'How did you even recognize them?'

'They were here before, about a month back. Aman Gupta, I think, one of the guys' names was. They said WTIC is planning to acquire BSD.'

I thought about this.

'You saw the BSD managers here, in the lab, today?'

'Yes, pretty sure it was them.'

'So, they are not in the small building, with the white guys?' Malini asked.

'No. But they may not be in the lab now anyway. It's late.'

'We should call Raj,' Malini said.

'Can I take a look at the cemetery now?' I asked.

Knight looked at me like I was crazy.

'You want to go visit the ghosts?' he said.

I gestured at Sathish. 'You have not seen him in action.'

'You can go into the cemetery through the other side of the compound,' he said. 'There is a small gate.'

'They have security there?'

He shook his head. 'You need to be crazy to go in through that gate. It is protected by the spirits.'

'Yes, okay.'

I nodded at Malini. 'Can you stay here? I'll go check this out. If Raj calls, tell him to come out.'

I got out of the car.

'Don't play the hero,' Knight said.

I stepped into the bushes to the left of the road.

Although I had put on a brave face in the car, and felt I could do more in this adventure than sit and wait for Raj to issue commands, my heart was hammering as I walked along the small grove that bordered WTIC. It was private land, but with no fences. Small animals skittered away as I walked and I was aware of the inadequate protection that my slippers provided.

I kept the tallest WTIC building as my guide as I walked. There was no moon that night. It was probably the new moon day – familiar to spirits of the underworld.

The tall wall with glass shards on top was to my right. As I got closer and closer, I could see it through the thorn bushes.

I continued to walk, looking carefully for the gate – Knight had said I could easily miss it. After about ten minutes I spotted it – a very tiny break, after which the wall resumed.

I went straight for it. The opening was small – only a

couple of people could walk through it. It had a rusty gate, on which there was no lock.

I opened it slowly. It creaked.

I waited to see if someone would come running.

No one did, but I suddenly felt the same strong sensation of someone standing behind me as I had at Malini's house.

I ignored it and opened the gate a little wider. Now, I could step through it.

I was in the WTIC campus.

It was not very dark here. I could see the buildings, a little farther away. In front of me the grove continued.

I stumbled on something and almost fell. I turned around, expecting to see a stone, but could not make out anything in the dark.

I stepped forward and again stumbled over what I thought was a stone. I took out my mobile phone and switched on its display.

In the eerie light that emanated from it, I could see a small stone cross rearing up from the ground.

I turned around; there were more crosses.

I was in the cemetery.

I kept the phone on and walked past them, so intent on looking around that I almost crashed into a black wall in front of me.

The wall extended to either side. There were no windows.

I could hear the sound of the udukku now. I put my ear to the wall.

There was a faint throbbing from inside. I walked along the wall and when I reached the eastern edge, I turned with it. I could see that the building was almost square and very small – probably just two or three rooms.

I walked all the way along, keeping to the wall. Then I

turned on the southward wall and saw the door. There were no windows on all the three sides I had seen, but I could clearly see the door. The sense of someone watching me grew as I walked towards it. I resisted the impulse to turn back.

The door was a plain, wooden one, with a simple handle. I turned it and it opened smoothly.

The light from inside blinded me for a moment. I stayed to the side of the door and peeked in.

There was a corridor, south to north, ending at the opposite wall. There were two rooms on either side. The sound of the udukku was coming from the right. I could hear some chanting along with it.

I was surprised that no one had stopped me till now. The whole building seemed deserted.

My hair stood on end as I slowly walked up the corridor and opened the first door to the left.

It was dark. I opened the door wide, with my heart beating so loud, they could probably hear it in the next building.

The walls of the room were painted black and in the centre of the room there was a recliner, actually, more like a dentist's chair, raised, with a flexible back. In front of it there was a monitor. There were tubes snaking around it, and it was attached to the ground through what looked like a hydraulic pulley system. A thin glittering cord lay in the centre of the recliner. My eyes followed its loops to where it was attached to the ceiling.

On the ceiling was painted an enormous yellow bright eye that glowed.

The sight sent a chill through me for some reason, and I hastily backed out and closed the door.

What was this room for, I wondered. It did actually look like a laboratory.

I stared at the door opposite, from where I could hear the chanting. The voice was now rising and falling, melodious, beckoning at this point. I resisted the urge to rush into that room though, for the silver cord had created a mindless fear in me.

Instead, I walked on and opened the door of the second room to the left.

It was a brightly lit, modern conference room. Four people were sitting around the table, and they all now had their eyes on me.

I pushed the door further and stepped in.

'Hi,' I said to Aman.

12

THE DEAL

My EXM teammates from that morning stared at me as if I were an apparition. All of them were there: Keerthi, Madhan, Aman and Dileepan.

'Arjun? What are you doing here?' Aman asked.

I hesitated. I had come into this building expecting Aman and the rest to be either bound physically or being subjected to some cruel experiment by Anderson. I expected that they would be relieved when they saw me.

Instead, they looked startled, and guilty.

'I came here looking for you,' I said.

'But . . .' Aman said, 'how did you find us? Why are you looking for us?'

I did not know how to answer this. I had spent the last eight hours moving heaven and earth trying to find and save these guys. A horrible thought crossed my mind.

'You have no idea that I'm still working for you?' I said, incredulous.

They all looked at me with open mouths.

'After Sathish escaped . . .' I said, 'you expected me to go home and quit?'

Madhan shrugged and said, 'That is what we expected, from your personality profile. You were not expected to do anything, nor did you need to.'

Aman raised a hand to silence him.

'What personality profile?' I said. 'What the hell? Do you at least know that Anderson has been communicating with me?'

They looked surprised.

'No, why. We are all right here,' said Keerthi.

I slapped my palm on my head.

'You are all here, talking with Anderson?'

'Yes, we are negotiating things and we may have a solution soon,' smiled Madhan.

I looked at all of them. How could I have been so stupid? Of course they negotiated after Sathish left – that is what managers do. They thought they had lost all their cards. Nobody had considered that I would step in and get Sathish back.

I breathed deeply. The door was still open. I closed it, walked to a chair and collapsed into it.

Anderson had reeled me in, along with Sathish, by pretending that Aman and the others were in his control.

I realized that Malini could be in danger, so close to the WTIC office. Maybe I should call her and ask her to leave.

The door opened and the man I had seen that morning in the IIT campus walked in. He was alone, and he came in smiling. He did not seem at all surprised to see me.

'Hi Arjun,' he said. 'We meet again. I'm Anderson.'

I abandoned the thought of calling Malini. Anderson did not yet know, I assumed, that she was close by, with Sathish.

He extended his hand. I reached across and shook it.

'Apologies for this morning. I had not yet gotten your measure,' he said.

He nodded at the others. 'Do we have a deal?' he asked.

Aman looked embarrassed and avoided my eye.

'I think so,' he said finally.

I gathered some courage.

'What is the deal, Aman?' I asked.

'You do not need to know,' said Dileepan.

Anderson smiled at Dileepan. His eyes were dead.

'Arjun, here, has earned my respect,' he said. 'You should explain the deal to him.'

Dileepan went red.

'I can explain,' Aman said. 'We have the interests of our shareholders in mind, Arjun. You have to understand that. We have to answer to them. 'The terms of our agreement will be very beneficial to BSD. PH Capital has agreed to pump some much-needed cash into our company. They have also agreed to cease their hostilities in Ahi against us. What they cannot do is to free Sathish from the possession. They have expressed their regret, but they cannot really undo it without a backlash against themselves. We can all understand this.

'In return for their help, we have agreed to mitigate the fallout when the plan comes to light, which it will, eventually since Sathish has sent some documents to WikiLeaks. We have agreed that we will denounce any revelations from WikiLeaks and help protect the name of PH Capital. That is the deal, and I think it is fair.'

'What about the dead programmer?' I asked.

'Who?'

'Subbu, the programmer whom PH Capital killed.'

'Let's not get carried away. We do not know that he was killed,' started Madhan.

'Oh, he was killed all right,' I said. 'I saw the video.'

Anderson was silent. This must have come as news to him. I could not read anything from his face.

'For a village, you can lose a man,' said Keerthi. 'Subbu violated disclosure and client confidentiality. PH Capital had to protect their interests.'

I stared at her. Then I looked around the room.

These people were sociopaths, I realized. I was suddenly afraid for my life. The fear must have shown on my face, because Anderson smiled again.

My voice shook when I spoke. 'You are going to abandon your boss, forswear any loyalty. You are letting a set of killers go scot-free. You are also going to help unleash a deadly cyber attack that is going to raise oil prices and cripple the global economy, apart from causing explosions in refineries. You are willing to do all that for some cash infusion?'

'You are mistaken, Arjun,' Aman said calmly. 'Our loyalty is not to Sathish. Nor is it to Subbu or the global economy. Our loyalty is to the shareholders. We do whatever it takes to keep the company afloat. That is our mandate.'

I remained silent.

'I think Arjun is missing a small piece of this puzzle,' said Anderson. He sat down and crossed his legs.

'This program, Blaze, is important to us, Arjun. A lot of people in my company have bet on rising oil prices. Unfortunately, the prices have stayed low. Blaze was our idea to manage this situation. Billions of dollars is in play. Do you know what Sathish actually did, given these stakes?' he asked.

I shook my head.

'The programmer Subbu went to Sathish and told him about our . . .' he hesitated, 'plans for the Blaze program. If

Sathish had reservations, he could have raised them with us, his clients. Instead, he sent all our internal communications about Blaze and its full specifications to WikiLeaks. The only reason they have not published it, is because they could not verify the authenticity. We could have eliminated him just for that.' Anderson smiled.

'Instead you chose to drive him insane, so that the leaks would be dismissed as coming from a crazy man,' I said.

'Correct.'

'And now Aman and the others will help you dismiss him publicly. That is the deal?' I said.

'Yes. You are remarkable,' he said.

I was silent. What could I say?

'Now, we have a small glitch in the sequence of events,' said Anderson. 'According to the terms of the deal, you have to hand Sathish over to us. We have plans for him, this evening. Our Sathish is going to be on television,' he said and laughed.

'Where is Sathish?' Aman asked Andersen. 'We thought you had him.'

'Nope. Your man here has him somewhere.'

They all gaped at me.

Anderson got up. Slowly he walked around the room and stood behind me.

'I am amazed, Arjun, that you traced us here. I thought you might have the motivation, but I was not sure of your ability,' he said.

Here come the fireworks, I thought.

'I'm sure we can persuade Arjun, Mr Anderson,' Aman said.

Anderson laughed softly.

'Believe me, Aman, my persuasive powers are a lot better than yours.'

He turned the chair so that I faced him.

'Did you see the chair in the next room?' he asked.

I nodded.

'Do you know we treated Sathish in it? It was a special twenty-four hour treatment. They could hear his screams in the main building.'

I stayed silent.

'But, maybe,' Anderson continued, 'maybe you will see reason. I am not sure why you are still engaged in this dispute between PHC and BSD. You cannot do more than you have already done. Can we offer you something, some position in the new BSD?'

I hesitated. Could I use this to get out of here?

'You will be a valuable asset,' he said.

I decided to keep mum.

The door opened and one of the guys who had come to pick us up at the restaurant walked in.

'They seem to have triangulated us with the drone signal,' he told Anderson.

Anderson gestured at me. 'You want to try him, Steve?' he said.

'Gladly, boss,' Steve said and came around the table. He leaned forward and took out his gun.

'Shoot off his knee?' he asked.

'Whatever,' said Anderson.

Steve turned the gun around so he was holding it by its nozzle, and then hit me across the face. I jerked back, failed to avoid the blow, and caught it full force on my lips. I heard a scream and realized it was me. I saw blood on my shirt as I bent down and tried not to choke.

'Do you know why these guys chose you for their team, Arjun?' Andersen asked.

My head was pounding and I felt ready to retch.

'Do we need to do this here?' Aman said.

'Blood makes you queasy?' Anderson asked. 'Come on, tell him why you chose him for your team.'

'It is not what you think, Arjun.' Aman's voice oozed sympathy.

'They chose you because you have no family. The plan was to sacrifice you to Vellaya Thevan tonight. Did you know that, Arjun?'

I could feel tears flowing down my face. They stung my lower lip. It must have split open.

'They planned to kill you to save Sathish. How does that make you feel?' jeered Anderson.

'Let's just kill him,' said Steve. 'We can find the crazy bastard by ourselves.'

The pain was unbearable. I slowly looked up. Aman turned away.

There go my chances for marriage, I thought.

Someone knocked on the door.

Anderson turned, surprised. He stepped away from me and opened the door.

There was a guy standing there. He seemed scared already but he went pale when he saw me.

'What is it?' snapped Anderson.

'Someone left you a message,' said the new guy.

'What? What kind of message?'

The new guy held out a paper. 'Someone named Raj came in to help us with the code. He asked me to give this to you.'

Anderson looked puzzled. 'You brought someone in to fix the code? Where is this guy?'

'I don't know where he went. He dropped in an hour back.'

'And you just showed him the code?' Anderson asked, disbelieving.

The guy shuffled around, looking trapped. He kept glancing over at me.

'Stay outside,' Andersen said, and closed the door in his face. Then he opened out the paper and read through it. Confusion and then rage spread through his face.

He looked at me after finishing the message.

'This Raj, your friend?'

I kept silent.

'Wow,' he said waving the message. 'I'm impressed. Read this.' He tossed the paper to me.

I picked it up with shaking hands and read.

Dear Mr Anderson,

You have a problem with the Blaze code. I can do you a favour and fix the problem. Nobody else can fix it – the bug was put in by a very smart programmer. I have the source files.

As a way to return the favour, please let Arjun out. I want to see him walk out of WTIC with no visible harm done.

If I do not see him out in half an hour, your code will be broken irrevocably. I will destroy the source files.

Regards

Raj

I shook my head and read it again.

If Anderson agreed, Raj may well end up dead. He probably knew that and was sacrificing himself.

Anderson opened the door and grabbed the guy standing outside by his arm. He dragged him in.

'Listen, moron,' he said, 'we have a problem with the code and you never told us?'

'I did tell you in the last status update,' the project manager squeaked.

'But didn't the code work when we released to that refinery at Jeddah?'

'Yes, but it is not working in live.'

'You knew about this earlier? And you hid it from me?'

'The last status update . . .' began the manager. Anderson slapped him. The manager took a couple of steps back and almost fell down. He looked thoroughly humiliated.

'Get the hell out,' said Anderson.

The manager ran out.

Anderson's cool façade seemed to have been breached. He looked around distractedly.

'I should kill all of you,' he said pointing at Aman. 'That is what I wanted, not stupid negotiations.'

He turned away, visibly trying to calm himself down.

'All right,' he rubbed his hands together, 'I'm letting you go now. But before this day is out, you will hear from me,' he said.

I got up. My lower lip felt like it had grown ten times its original size. I walked past Steve and Anderson, opened the door and staggered out.

∞

I stood at the gates of WTIC, thinking that Raj must be watching from somewhere. Anderson's guys were also probably watching me.

I started walking along the highway. It helped clear my mind. The cool night air chilled the wound on my face.

Anderson had been given two tasks: to stop Sathish, or ruin his reputation; and to release the virus so that it would do maximum damage to oil prices. He wanted to accomplish both. Now he had been cornered to choose between them. He did not like that, but he probably had no choice until Raj fixed the code.

That gave me a few hours. What should I do?

The dark bushes on either side of the road threatened me.

A car came speeding through the night. It slowed down near me. Akram's Pajero.

'Jump in,' said Akram.

I opened the front door and dived in. The car raced away.

I kept my face averted. 'What happened,' I mumbled.

'Sorry?' Malini said.

'Blap blahned?' I repeated.

'I can't understand what you're saying. What happened to you?'

Akram slowed the car and said, 'Dude, you're creeping us out. Can you turn towards me?'

I turned and looked at him.

'Jesus,' he said. So it was bad. I turned back to look at Malini. She flinched. That hurt more.

'Nothing cosmetic surgery cannot fix,' I said. It came out garbled.

Then I tried smiling.

Malini looked sick. 'Oh, you poor man,' she said.

I turned away and said again, 'What happened?' I found that talking with a weight tied to one lip was a challenge. I could enunciate only if I spoke from the corner of my mouth.

'Should we go to a doctor?' Akram asked.

'No time,' I said.

'What happened after I left?'

'Oh, you're asking what happened!' said Malini. I nodded vigorously.

'That guy Knight left. Then Raj came out. He was all

agitated. He said it was a trap, that your BSD colleagues were safe. We told him you went to the cemetery. He asked us to leave and said he was going back into the building. Did you see him?'

I shook my head.

'What happened to you?'

I explained painfully the details of my mutilation.

'Raj is now in there fixing their code?' Malini asked.

I nodded.

'But he may be killed once he is done.'

'Yes. I know.'

Malini went silent.

'He was a good man, a hero,' I said.

Nobody replied.

'We have to continue,' I said. 'I have decided to do my part.'

I picked up my phone and dialled Idumban.

'I'm ready to go to Ahi,' I said when he picked up.

13

THE WORLD OF AHI

'I cannot be driving you guys around forever,' Akram said.

'One last time,' I said. 'This is on your way.'

Idumban had given us instructions to a place near the Pallikaranai marsh. We had been that way earlier that night, on our way to Subbu's home.

Idumban had had some difficulty understanding me. Before he hung up, he had insisted that I bring Sathish when I came.

'Get down near the second bus stop,' he had said. 'Wait for me.'

There had been no communication from Raj. I texted him, but got no reply.

The car turned into the road cutting through the marsh. It was very dark here. We drove slowly, counting the bus stops. There were several notice boards about the birds that nested in the marsh.

If there was a police patrol around we would be in trouble.

We slowly rolled up to the second bus stop. I got down first. Malini followed me.

'You should leave with Akram,' I told her.

She shrugged. 'I cannot really go back at this hour. Who knows, I may even be of use to you.'

After Akram had left we waited in the dark for Idumban. I looked at Malini. What was she doing here? It took extraordinary bravery to be here, at this time of the night. Why was she here?

After a couple of minutes, we could see someone walking towards us in the dark. It was a tall man. He had a staff in one hand and a torchlight in the other. He tapped the staff on the ground as he walked. He stopped a short distance away and said, 'Arjun?'

'Yes. Are you Idumban?'

'Follow me,' he said.

Malini and I supported Sathish and we hobbled along behind Idumban.

After five minutes, he turned right into the marsh. An odd smell assaulted us. I could see a small path through the bushes on the edge of the marsh.

The smell became stronger as we walked. I could see smoke billowing in the distance. Ahead of us was a small wooden fence and a gate that lay open. He walked through it.

I realized that we were in a crematorium. An owl hooted in the distance. The smell must be of burning bodies.

I wanted to object, but was afraid of opening my mouth. I had no intention of provoking any spirits tonight. I wondered if they could smell blood.

The path split and Idumban took the right. A little distance away, I could see a hut with a thatched roof.

This guy seemed to be a real sorcerer.

He stopped in front of the door, fumbled with the lock and then turned to us.

'Please come in,' he said.

We all had to bend down and drag Sathish in.

Idumban sat down cross-legged in the centre of the room.

'Sit down,' he said.

We lay Sathish down and sat next to him. I was tired from the walking.

The hut was spacious inside. There were a couple of yellow light bulbs hanging from the ceiling. Several boxes lined the walls, and there were a couple of bookshelves crammed with hardbound volumes.

What surprised me was the painting on the ceiling. It was the same one I had seen in the cemetery lab – a glowing yellow eye.

Idumban looked at us closely, first focusing on Malini. This was not surprising, because she managed to look ethereal in the middle of the night in a crematorium. Then he looked at me, and I showed him my full frontal face. That would teach him, I thought.

He leaned forward and stared at the injury.

'That's a beauty,' he said. 'Hold on.' He went to a corner of the hut, fished around in a box and then came back with what I assumed was magic elixir.

'What is this? Ancient remedy of the sages?' I asked.

'No, tincture,' he replied. Before I could move away, he had applied the burning hot chemical on my lips. I yelled out in agony.

'There,' he said. 'You will be fine.'

'You have a first aid kit here?' Malini asked.

He looked at her bound arm. 'Should I take a look at that?' he said.

'No, the knife just grazed me.'

'You are a brave woman,' he said. 'Worthy descendant of Vellaya Thevan.'

'You know about him?' she asked.

'I have spoken to him,' he said calmly.

A chill ran down my spine.

Malini laughed. 'You are not two hundred years old,' she said.

'No, of course not. Believe me, I wish I lived in his time. Inspiring man.'

'Can we leave for Ahi?' I said.

He turned his attention to me. 'We?'

'Aren't you coming? We don't have transport,' I said.

He laughed a deep laugh. 'Unfortunately,' he said, 'I cannot come with you there. And you do not need transportation. You will just go through the silver cord.'

I felt another chill. I remembered the thin silver cord lying on the torture chair.

He nodded as if he had read my thoughts.

'Ahi is not in this world,' he said.

My day was now complete. I seemed to have volunteered for a trip straight to hell.

'You will find out shortly,' he continued. 'Now, can you describe what happened with Aman and the others?'

I narrated, slowly and painfully, our efforts to locate Anderson. He listened patiently, and interrupted me only once.

'You saw a chair with a silver cord?' he asked.

'Yes.'

His face clouded over.

'And Anderson said he used that on Sathish?'

'Yes. He said Sathish's screams could be heard in the main building.' I then explained that Aman had decided to reach a deal with Anderson.

'There goes my payment,' Idumban said.

Malini thought that was very funny.

I said, 'When they were working on my face, Anderson said something. He said I was meant to be sacrificed to Vellaya Thevan tonight.'

'Yes.'

'That is true?'

'It is an experimental idea. Your guys wanted that. They said they could find someone from their payroll, a person without a family. Someone without attachments, whom they could use.'

'Use for what?'

Idumban sighed.

'Arjun, the sorcery business is complicated. It is going through a great transition because of companies like WTIC and PH Capital. I come from a family of sorcerers. My father wanted me to continue in the line. I rejected him and became a physician instead.'

'Alternative medicine?'

'No, regular medicine. I hold an MD degree in Neurology from the University of California medical school.'

'You're kidding me!' I said.

'No. I have my degree somewhere in those boxes. It's pretty much useless.'

'Why would you come back and . . .' I gestured around at the hut, 'live here?'

'I specialized in neurology, as I said. Do you know what Ahi is, Arjun? Anyone explain to you yet?'

'Some kind of scary underworld?'

Idumban stood up. The top of his head almost hit the roof.

'Nobody knows what happens after death,' he said, beginning to pace the room. 'It's something that happens to every living thing, in some form. Evolutionary biologists have puzzled over it for the last fifty years. Ideally, death should have been eliminated by natural selection. If evolution could create something as complex as the human brain, surely it could eliminate death.

'It is a question that led to investigations of NDEs, near-death experiences. Another track went through neurology, to figure out what happens to the brain when one dies. Throughout history, there have been ideas of the afterlife. It's existed as a concept in the Vedas; in Buddhism; for the Jews and Arabs; the Mayans, Egyptians, Greeks, the Norse tribes – all of them had elaborate myths of a world after death. We called it the Vritra Loka, or Ahi. The Greeks had Hades. The Norsemen called it Valhalla.

'Science, of course, dismisses an afterlife. No theory can be formed on it because the concept of afterlife is not falsifiable. Modern science does have an explanation for death – when you die, you die. That is it. There is no soul. And science is, indeed, correct. I do not think there is a soul either.'

'You mean you are an atheist?'

'Yes.'

'So how come you're speaking with dead people?' Malini asked.

'Good question. To understand that, you have to go back to what my family and other sorcerers have been doing for thousands of years. People like my father could communicate with dead people. They brought peace to the dead person's families. But there has always been a dark side to the profession. I've seen men and women driven insane by the work of a sorcerer. I rejected this in my teens and left the family profession.

'While I was working in the US, there was new interest in NDEs. Also, brain-mapping techniques were being tested out to chart different areas of the human brain. One such test is documented in this book,' he said and grabbed a bound journal from one of the bookshelves.

'In this particular test, they had attached probes to different areas of the brain for stimulation. One particular area, called Broca's region, is meant for language cognition. The experiment was to find out what happened if some points in this area were stimulated. The doctor meant to find that the patient would talk, or recognize something.

'Instead, while probing one particular area, the doctor felt, in *his* mind, an image pop up.

'You can imagine how shocked he must have been. This article states that he tried this experiment on different people; and different labs redid it. They always found that the tester had reactions when a subject was probed.

'You can understand what that eventually meant, right?' he asked us.

'No,' I said.

'Yes,' said Malini. 'It means telepathy exists.'

'Correct,' he beamed at Malini. 'It meant that there was some capability to communicate from one human brain to another. Also, this facility exists only in human brains, since language is specific to humans. Intense excitement was generated by this experiment. Some neurologists work on detecting the electromagnetic waves from brains. They showed that there is a default frequency that emanates even when we are asleep.

'Unfortunately, the telepathic ability could not be used

at all consciously. In other words, human brains had the ability to communicate with each other, but did so in some mysterious fashion that we could never use consciously. In one intuitive leap, an American neurologist postulated a hypothesis, about what this telepathy means. He linked it with death and the afterlife.'

He showed me the journal.

It was the science magazine *Nature*. The title of the article was, *The serialization of human consciousness at death*.

It was authored by one Mr Idumban Kaari.

∾

'The reason I could solve the puzzle of unconscious telepathy, was because I came from a sorcery background,' said Idumban. 'I had experienced, as a young kid, this telepathy in sleep. I could hear voices and see identities of long dead people, in my mind. Through college, I was afraid that I was schizophrenic. I took multiple tests to make sure I was not mentally ill. When the results of the Broca's area telepathy came out, I rejected it at first, like most of my colleagues. But I changed my mind soon, as more confirmation came in. Nobody could ignore these experiments. I worked on a few subjects myself, and realized that there is indeed such communication.

'My theory was developed over ten years. I reasoned that evolution had indeed tried to eliminate death. The human brain had developed a means of establishing not just communication, but, more importantly, a network. This network runs like the computer networks of our times – it sustains even if we die, on living people's minds. The brain simply serializes identity and memory into this network, at the time of death. If you are successful at this, you live on, in the network. If you fail, then you die. You really die – no soul exists.'

'You are saying the human brain evolved telepathy just so it could live after death?' asked Malini.

'Yes,' he said.

'This network exists through all our brains?'

'Yes. It is a collective space. If all humans die, there will be no network and no Ahi Loka. The Ahi Loka depends on human brains to network. This results in some interesting problems, but you will learn that when you go in there,' he said, to me.

'Listen, I really do not want to die,' I said.

'You do not have to. There are two ways to get in there. Both go through a virtual silver cord that links you to the network. One way is through death, but the silver cord will be cut and you cannot come back.'

'What is the other way?' I asked.

'You get high,' he said.

'Ganja?'

'No, there is another, more powerful drug that helps you get into alien worlds. It is called dimethyl triptamine, DMT,' he said, bending down and picking up his staff.

'Let's go,' he said, walking towards the door.

'Where are we going?' I asked.

'To get DMT. We have to collect it from the sorcerers' council,' he said, opening the door. 'They control the drug's distribution.'

I just wanted to curl up and sleep in the hut. Malini looked exhausted too.

I got up, aching in every limb.

'Do you have a car? How far is this place?' I asked him.

'It is on the beach, half an hour's drive,' he said. 'Today is the new moon, so the council may all be there. We may even be able to meet the council head.'

'Yay,' I said.

We walked outside again. Idumban went behind the hut and dragged out an ancient Vespa scooter with a sidecar.

'Make yourselves comfortable,' he said.

We stared at the scooter. It was dirty and looked like it may have creepy crawly things under the seats. The cushions were torn.

He got on and waited for us. I helped put Sathish in the side car. Malini squeezed in next to him. I sat behind Idumban.

He kick-started the scooter. It made a loud sound, sputtered a few times and then finally caught on.

'Here we go,' he said. The scooter rattled through the ditches in the crematorium and roared out onto the main road.

❧

As we were bumping along the road to the beach, I thought about what I had just heard.

Idumban had provided an explanation for the existence of life after death. It seemed that life existed in a network sustained by human brains.

And he said he had spoken with Vellaya Thevan. If what he was saying was true, then there were actual dead people, or their consciousness, roaming around within our minds.

That was scary.

I remembered my childhood experience – the one time I had felt the presence of a spirit and heard it snarl in the feverish night.

Was that from an actual dead person? Why was he haunting me? Was he still hanging around my mind?

Was my father in Ahi?

The cold November air blew through my hair.

My father had died cursing me. Coughing and heaving from tuberculosis, he still managed to curse me for his life's problems.

We had no money. None for his treatment; none for my education. I had just finished high school and was running from one relative to another, begging, pleading for any crumbs we could get.

Nobody cared.

In the end, my father died in the crumbling house where we had ended up. The previous day he had accused me of hoarding money for college, the good life, and women. Anything but for him.

I had sat next to him, staring at my school books.

He was in a coma now, and I could hear the death rattle in his breath.

Then it stopped.

I wondered how the dead people in Ahi felt about the live ones. Did my father still think I was a useless bastard? Did he watch over me? Was he even interested in my existence?

If this afterlife actually existed, then I could understand what had happened to Sathish. Someone had sent the spirit of Vellaya Thevan after his mind. It made sense, if the network existed in the mind, that dead people could tunnel back in and influence living humans.

Even more scary.

Maybe my father was there, waiting to taunt me.

14

THE SORCERERS' COUNCIL

We reached a small grove, beyond which I could hear the sea. The scooter had listed dangerously to one side on our way through a small lane. It was a wonder that the police had not come chasing after us, with all the noise the scooter was making.

Idumban parked his scooter and we all got down and stretched.

'We have to hurry,' he said.

At that point I noticed that we had company. There were a couple of shadowy figures standing by the grove. I could see them because there was a weird light coming from the inside of the grove.

The figures kept watching us as we walked on the sand towards the grove. As we approached, I could see they were cloaked tall men – and not the ghosts I was afraid they would be.

From inside the grove came the chatter of many voices. We walked slowly, taking Sathish with us. Between the tall trees there were some lights that we could see now. Shadows crisscrossed the sand.

A little deeper into the grove there was some sort of a clearing. The lights were around this space. In the middle of it there were a few plastic chairs, looking completely out of place in the sinister setting. A few men sat on the ground in front of the chairs. Others were on the edges, groups of two or three, smoking and speaking softly amongst themselves.

It looked more like an apartment committee meeting than a powerful sorcerers' council.

The conversation stopped when our presence registered. Everyone stared at us. Idumban ignored them. We walked to a corner and sat down in the sand.

'There are women here,' whispered Malini.

It was true. Some of the people sitting were women. That made me more comfortable. Maybe they wouldn't all jump on Malini.

The group closest to us began chatting again.

'How often do you meet with the council?' I asked Idumban.

'Very rarely. I think this is my second or third time.'

'But, you said they need to provide the drug, DMT. Surely people need that drug all the time to get into Ahi.'

Idumban remained silent. Then he said, 'You are only the third person to go into Ahi, as far as I know.'

'You're joking. Who are the other two?'

'I was the first. I cannot go back there, because of an issue.'

'I see, who is the other one?'

'My son, Soman. You will meet him shortly.'

'Oh, sure, I look forward to it,' I said politely.

'You shouldn't really. He is going to try and kill you in Ahi.'

☙

There was someone shuffling towards us. It was a small man carrying a bag. He was going from one group to the other.

'You want our new drug?' he said reaching us. 'Can get lovers together. Potions, herbs, drugs – you want some?' he said.

'How are you, Thiru?' Idumban said.

'Oh, you, great,' Thiru said.

'Are they here?' whispered Idumban.

'Yes. I have not seen your son.'

'Do they have DMT?'

'Yes, freshly prepared for today. I think they will listen to you. It is just a formality.'

Thiru peered at me and Malini. He did a double take on seeing my mutilated face.

'Who is this man?' he asked.

Idumban laughed. 'New recruit,' he said.

After Thiru left Idumban explained to us: 'DMT cannot be hoarded. It degrades within a day. You need the right mix. The council now controls that mix. We have to convince them that we need it for a good purpose.'

'Do you trust them?' I asked. 'Maybe they're all corrupt. Most committees are corrupt.'

There was a small commotion to one side. Four men walked towards the chairs. They looked like Idumban – tall and dark with shawls wrapped around them.

I thought everyone would get up and say, 'Good morning, Sir', or something, but nothing happened. The people assembled on the sides came over and sat down. A few still chose to be cool and remain where they were, smoking.

The council took their seats. They conferred among themselves. One of them got up. He looked imposing, even taller than Idumban.

'Fellow sorcerers,' he said, in Tamil. 'Thank you for coming.'

He took a look around the clearing.

'This council has existed, as you know, for a thousand years. We trace our roots to the alchemists of the Cholas; the siddhas of the Pandyas; and the sages of the north. We have been sustained by the patronage of the gods. The adversities faced by these men are enormous. Society has shunned us. Few of us have married or had children to continue our lineage. Sorcerers have been burnt alive, and mounted on the stake. Our crime has been that we try and work with our brethren in the world of Ahi.

'In our thousand years of history, we have been declared done and finished many times over. But, in the end, we have emerged victorious. Again and again.

'In this age of modern science, we faced our biggest crisis. Many of us left the fold, disbelieving. The remaining spent their lives in self-doubt. Was all our work and history futile? Were our ancestors charlatans? Were we carrying a useless torch forward?

'The discovery of a scientific basis for Ahi, and the proof of its existence was soothing music to our ears. We have been vindicated, we thought. Our time had come, as practitioners of the Dark Arts. When the news spread through our small community here, and thousands such around the world, we breathed a collective sigh of relief. Our work had not been in vain. We anticipated more respect; and a better life for us.'

He paused.

'But, we had not thought of the forces of modern capitalism, and technology. This art, with its closely guarded wisdom; and ethical rules now faces its greatest threat, possibly in history. We, assembled here, and in these councils around the world, are now being corrupted from the inside.

'Corporations have invaded our space. They see Ahi and its denizens as new tools to be used in their various fights against each other, their governments and even their customers. A few of us see nothing wrong in working with them. We have heard disturbing rumours of experiments with the passage of the silver cord, in this very city. Our centuries-old secret potions have already been handed over to pharmas around the world. They have broken those down, and have re-engineered them in countless ways to the brave new world of mind control and other abominations.

'But, we in this council believe the corporations are evil; and they are out to destroy the way of our brethren in Ahi. We now hear of constant conflict in that world. We hear of panicked spirits despairing for oblivion. We do not know the causes for these conflicts, but we suspect the corporations have a role to play.

'At this juncture, we have received a request to supply the magic elixir of Drona, the drug DMT, for a trip to Ahi. The person who made the request, Idumban, wants to send a messenger to Ahi, and correct a grievous wrong. Where is Idumban?'

Idumban stood up.

'You all know him,' continued the council man. 'He is our man, son of Maaran, who went into the world of science and was victorious there too. Idumban, can you tell this council what you told me in private?'

Idumban cleared his throat.

'Two months back, when I was in meditation, a man

came to me from Ahi,' he started, speaking in Tamil as well. 'The man said there was an attempt to influence one of the esteemed demon leaders. They had felt several attempts by someone to get through from the Living world. The man had talked with the demon leader, Vellaya Thevan.'

The assembled crowd gasped.

'Yes,' said Idumban. 'The man who spoke to me said someone was trying to repeat the experiment I did ten years back. If you remember, I had made a trip to Ahi and barely managed to come back. The man asked me to check if someone was trying to get back into Ahi. He did not think Vellaya Thevan was making the correct decisions. I checked with my contacts in our group and could not find anything.

'After a month of these efforts, I was ready to give up. Then, I read and saw how a man named Sathish Kumar behaved at a conference. Sathish Kumar is the head of a software company called BSD in Chennai and his behaviour and some of the words he used in that incident convinced me that he was possessed. A possession in this day and age struck me as unusual. I connected this with the demon leader Vellaya Thevan and decided to contact BSD Technologies.

'At first contact they refused to believe me. But soon, I convinced them that Sathish was possessed. I got them to recover him physically and checked him. It seemed that Sathish had angered Vellaya Thevan. This anger was created and the possession caused by a sorcerer from our midst. He was the man who had gone into Ahi; the second person to have done so.'

'Who was the traitor?' exclaimed a man in front.

'We need not go into that,' said the council head.

Idumban raised his hand.

'I am ashamed to tell you, but it was my own son, Soman, whom you all know.'

There was a silence around the grove. We could hear the waves and the wind's murmur.

'My son, who had learnt the techniques of Ahi from my lap, has now gone over to the corporates. I apologize for him.'

The council head stepped in.

'To combat the possession, and check what is going on in Ahi, Idumban has a solution. He wants to send a man in to talk to Vellaya Thevan.'

'But that is suicidal,' said one of the sorcerers. 'He may not be able to get in, or even make contact. Vellaya Thevan may rip his limbs off.'

'I have found a brave man for this very purpose,' said Idumban.

I wanted to go to the bathroom.

'Hold on,' said another man. 'How are you going to send him without DMT?'

'That is why we are here. We wish to hand over the drug to Idumban. The council is in favour of it . . .'

'What??' yelled someone. 'How can you do that? His own son is guilty. What if the drug gets into the wrong hands?'

'Soman already has access to the drug,' said Idumban calmly. 'You have to trust me.'

Everyone started talking at the same time.

'You actually have DMT here?' yelled someone.

'Yes.'

'But, goddamnit, Soman may know we are meeting here,' said someone else.

'That is true,' said Idumban.

'True? What if he arrives . . .?'

There was a loud crack, a gunshot close to us.

A few men had materialized from the back of the grove. One of them had his hand raised; in it was a gun.

There was chaos as people screamed and tried to get away. A few ran straight to the opposite end of the clearing and were met by more men with guns.

The man with the gun stepped slowly into the circle of light. He was young, well-built, wearing jeans and a T-shirt. Dark as the night and handsome. The light threw shadows on his face.

'Hello, father,' he said.

Idumban remained immobile. I could not read his face.

'Everyone, sit down,' Soman commanded.

The sorcerers reluctantly came back and sat down. Idumban remained standing. So did the council head.

'Old men,' said Soman smiling. 'I was listening to this idiot talking,' he gestured towards the council head. 'You cannot fight the forces of nature. You should know that, of all people,' he said, looking around.

His voice was powerful and melodious.

'My father has given me this great opportunity to massacre all of you,' he said.

The council head said, 'Soman, you are breaking the law. You cannot get away with this.'

'Where is the DMT?' Soman said.

'You should leave now.'

Soman raised his gun.

'No,' yelled Idumban. 'Don't do it. He is protected.'

Soman smirked and shot the council head in the chest.

Blood shot out and the council man fell back on his

chair. The chair keeled over and he crumpled to the sand. There were more screams from the crowd.

As Soman turned to the other council men, I realized a strange thing. The world seemed to be spinning right under me. The grove was bathed in a bright light that grew more and more intense. I could hear people calling out to each other and suddenly it was as if the sea was upon us.

Then it was all dark.

15

THE SILVER CORD

Someone was shaking me. I opened my eyes with difficulty and sat up. I realized I must have lost consciousness.

We were still in the grove, but everything was silent. All the men and women around us were lying down, seemingly unconscious.

Idumban was slowly shaking Malini as well.

'What happened?' I asked. 'Where is Soman?'

'It was the effect of killing a protected man,' said Idumban. 'It created a mental tsunami and anyone close cannot bear it.'

'You mean it was all in the mind?'

'Yes.'

Malini sat up slowly.

'How come you're not unconscious?' I asked Idumban.

'I protected myself. So did those men,' he pointed.

The other council men were up and walking around, waking up the others.

'Where is Soman?'

'He is there, on the ground,' pointed Idumban.

I looked over and could see the men who had come with Soman sprawled on the ground.

I could not see Soman.

'He is not there,' I said.

Idumban did not seem too interested.

'We have to get the DMT and go,' he said.

One of the council men came to us and handed a bag to Idumban.

'Be careful,' he said.

He looked at me. 'You are a brave man. Good luck to you.'

I nodded.

We picked up Sathish and left the grove.

∽

Idumban was silent on the way back. I left him to his thoughts.

We reached the crematorium in Pallikaranai and made our way back to the hut. Idumban kept his staff in a corner and lay Sathish down on the ground. Malini sat next to Sathish. She looked very sleepy.

Idumban sat cross-legged on the floor and I sat facing him. He had a small set of utensils. While unwrapping the DMT, he broke his silence.

'You have to understand Ahi. You will need help there. I cannot get in, but I know a man who can help,' he said.

'A man in Ahi? A dead man?'

'Yes. His name is Veer. You must go meet him right away.'

'Hold on. Back to basics,' I said. 'What does Ahi look like? How do I go from one place to another there? Does it have space-time?'

Idumban smiled. 'All good questions. I went there ten years back on another mission. I will explain what it's like.'

He started mixing the DMT with some potion.

'Remember, no one knows when Ahi was formed. Nobody knows how far back the network developed. I have tried to collect bits and pieces of their history, but there are different versions.

'After it was formed, isolated communities sprang up, almost in islands. They do have a shared geography, but it is subject to disturbances in the network. Entire communities will disappear because the network had a glitch.

'To battle this, they wanted to achieve some stability. In reality, the network stability depends on the human mind's stability. For example, the world wars were disastrous for Ahi.

'Imagine you are a resident of Ahi. You have no idea how you got there. You try to establish some contact with other residents. You build relationships and a community. And then, one day, poof, all of that is gone when the network ruptures. You never know when that can happen.

'It is to combat such instability that the demons were formed. You will learn their history later, but there are many demon leaders. They were once tasked with monitoring human society, and even intervene if someone acts to create instability.

'Vellaya Thevan is a brave man. My suspicion is that he has been misled to possess Sathish. He must believe that Sathish is a danger to humanity, for some reason. You have to find that reason.'

'You mean I walk up to him and ask him?'

'That may not work,' said Idumban cautiously. 'He will probably recognize that you are a man not yet dead. Your silver cord will not be cut and that makes it easy to identify you as a non-resident of Ahi. He may suspect your motives.

'But, as I said, a man named Veer can help you. You have to reach him first. You asked about space-time. It exists in a certain form in Ahi. The place you land in will be near the castle of Panchala. I can try to get you as close as possible.

'The time you spend in there is about the same as the time in this world. So, you have to act fast. Remember, PH Capital and Soman do not know where I am right now. They will be looking for us. If they find me when you are in Ahi, you will be toast. You have to exorcise Sathish; get Vellaya Thevan out of his mind as soon as possible.'

'Anderson wants to put Sathish in front of the television cameras tonight,' I said.

Idumban thought about this.

'Yes, that would be disaster,' he said. 'He does not have Sathish right now, but who knows what will happen in the next few hours. You may even end up being successful.'

Thanks for the vote of confidence, I thought.

'If Anderson has Sathish, maybe he will keep away from you,' Idumban said pensively.

'We have already sacrificed too many people in this,' I said.

He did not reply.

The hour had come. Idumban had given me instructions on how to find Veer.

I lay down on the floor. The ceiling lights were bright on my face. Idumban switched off one of them. He covered my body with a blanket.

I turned to look at Malini. She was fast asleep.

Idumban peered at me.

'When you see the bright light, stay away from it,' he said. 'It will pull you, but stay on your course.'

He stuck a needle in my arm. The thick, black liquid swirled into my blood stream.

I stared at the ceiling, at the silver cord and the bright light. Nothing happened for a few moments.

Then I felt my eyes get heavy.

I closed them. The silver cord faded away. But it was still bright.

I felt as light as a feather. I was falling, within my own consciousness, deeper and deeper.

I could see dark walls rise on both sides – rough-hewn walls of stone. They kept rising as I fell within myself. I could hear a rushing sound now, like a falling cataract. The sound grew and pounded in my head.

The silver cord rose up in front of me, with an astral light around it. It glowed in the dark, and I felt myself being pulled in, head first. The cord grew bigger until I could see a long tunnel. The tunnel's walls were glowing, and as I got sucked in, I could see the bright light.

My life flashed in front of my eyes – here my childhood friend; here my first sight of the sea; there my father's raised belt; there his racking cough.

I watched fascinated as the bright light at the end of the tunnel grew in size.

I felt a great reluctance to continue along my course. Maybe it was time to leave. Just quit. The light bathed me in its sweet, warm light.

With great effort I turned away, and floated on in the cord. There was a whooshing sound, a bunch of bright flashes, and then it went dark.

PART II

THE WORLD OF AHI

*But for him who is joined to all the living there is hope,
for a living dog is better than a dead lion. For the living know
that they will die; but the dead know nothing, and they have no more
reward, for the memory of them is forgotten. Also their love, their
hatred, and their envy have now perished; nevermore will they have a
share in anything done under the sun.*

— Ecclesiastes 9:4-6

16

THE VAJRA

One day, a few men brought a speechless, sleeping man to Veer, of Panchala. They had never seen a sleeping man in Ahi, so they were puzzled. They thought he was faking at first. They had prodded him and laughed.

But much time passed, and he did not get up. They did not know any measure of time, so they decided to consult the wisest man, as protocol demanded. They carried him over to the house of Veer.

The house was just outside the castle of Panchala. It was tiny and sparse, and stood in the middle of a small grove, where strange plants grew. The light dimmed there, and there was a narrow babbling brook.

Veer was sitting down, cross-legged, on a rock by the brook. He was staring at the water when he heard them approach.

He stood up and waited for them.

They lay the man on the ground. One person explained what had happened. He seemed close to tears. The sleeping man was their close companion. They had spent many years in Ahi together.

Veer sat down by the sleeping man and touched his forehead. Then he ran his hand up and down the man's body. He lifted his shirt and probed. Then he stopped.

He undid the man's shirt, and there, on his chest, they could all see a mark. A mark like a puncture wound. It was a round hole.

Veer stood up shaking his head.

'What is that? Is he ill?' asked the companion. Illness was unknown in Ahi.

Veer said, in a clear voice, 'He is dead.'

They all looked at him without comprehension.

'How could he die? We all died once,' one of them said.

'Yes. Now he has left Ahi. He does not exist anymore,' said Veer.

The men muttered to one another. One of them knelt by the dead man and kissed his cheek.

'He is not coming back?' asked another.

'No.'

They did not have tears. They clustered around the dead man and kept touching him.

Veer asked them, 'Where was he? When did you last see him?'

Having got the answers, he left for the castle on a small horse.

Arjun Palani opened his eyes. He was lying on his back. It was dark, but he could see a glow of light ahead.

He could feel his body. It was intact. There floor below him seemed rough.

He sat up. The glow was coming from an opening in front of him. As his eyes became used to the dark, he could see that he was in a small cave-like structure. The light was probably the cave's opening.

The roof of the cave was not very high. He stood up, bending slightly. His clothes felt wet. His feet were bare and the floor beneath was wet too.

Out of curiosity, he turned to look behind him. The cave was not very deep. He could see a yawning chasm at its end. A shudder went through him. Idumban had told him about this gap. To get back to the world of the Living, to his own mind, he would have to fall through this abyss; if he was able to ever come back here.

He turned towards the cave opening and walked across the floor. The opening was a small crack, and he wedged himself through it.

He was on top of a small hill. The world of Ahi was spread out in front of him.

Veer was at the castle entrance, still astride his horse. There were several people going back and forth at the drawbridge. Trying to keep busy in a world that was beyond time.

The drawbridge looked worn out. The moat was dry. The bridge had not been raised since he had last visited, awhile ago.

He walked the horse slowly into the castle. There were guards on both sides, but no one checked him. They did not check anyone.

The spire of Panchala towered over the walls of the castle, the top – in the shape of an outstretched hand that reached up to the shapeless skies – glowing in the light.

Veer guided his horse along the paved street, straight to the chief of guard's office.

The chief was in there, looking busy. He glanced at Veer impatiently.

'What brings you here?' he asked.

Veer sat down in a chair. He hesitated for a moment and then said, 'Where is Vellaya Thevan?'

'Not your business,' said the chief.

'Is he in the castle?'

'I won't tell you.'

Veer sat immobile, staring at the ground. Then he said, 'I think you should strengthen the castle defences.'

The chief leaned back and guffawed.

'We can withstand any offence, old man,' he said.

'There has been a dismemberment,' said Veer.

'A what?'

'A dismemberment. A man was brought dead to my home today.'

The chief's eyes narrowed.

'How can that be? How can someone die in Ahi?'

'Yes. Good question. It has not happened in my lifetime here. But I have read about it. It is not good for us. Someone has the weapon to kill, a Vajra. You have to protect the castle.'

'Can I look at this man?' asked the chief.

'Sure. But we are losing time. I think you should stay here and take care of the castle. Let me go out and track down the weapon.'

'Who made you in charge around here?' said the chief. 'Aren't you folk,' he gestured with his hand, 'the ones who know the Vajra? You have the secret knowledge. Why shouldn't I arrest you?'

Veer was silent. Then he got up and left.

❧

On the dusty road to the citadel of Panchala, there is a small wayside inn. It is a short distance away, but the tall spire of Panchala is not visible at all.

Arjun had walked for a couple of hours to reach the inn. Idumban had told him that the siddha, Veer, could be there, partaking of their excellent stimulants.

At first, it surprised him that there were stimulants to consume in a world that existed in the collective mind, a world that was not 'real'. But then everything about this new world was puzzling. He had seen a couple of horses on the way. Why did they exist here? But there they were, plodding along the dirty road.

Ahi was gray. He had looked up at the sky and seen neither the sun nor the moon. It was just gray, as Earth would be on a cloudy day. There was enough light to see ahead, but where that light came from, he could not tell.

Apart from the horses, the road had been largely empty. He had been petrified of seeing a dead person for the first time, but it did not even register when he saw a group of men and women. They had looked at him curiously, but said nothing.

Idumban had warned him that Soman would follow him into Ahi. 'He may try to block you from seeing Vellaya Thevan. Stay away from him, because he is ruthless,' he had said.

Arjun stood outside the inn and looked to either side. The road to Panchala went past in a straight line. He could not see anyone on the road now.

The inn looked like a crypt. There was no sign or anything on top. He opened the door and stepped in.

A few men and women sat around in dim light, chatting. No one was drinking or eating.

Some of them turned to look at Arjun as he came in. He went up to a chair and sat down.

In one corner, there were three young men. They were whispering amongst themselves, and paid no attention to him.

Closer to him, there were a couple of old men and a woman. They were looking at him with frank interest.

'You look young,' said one of the men in Tamil. 'New around these parts?'

Arjun looked down at himself. He was wearing the same clothes as in the real world. The men looked different. They wore dhotis and were shirtless. They looked like the old people he'd seen sitting around in temples.

'Yes, I am new,' he said.

'Aha! It is a long time since we saw someone new around these parts,' said the woman.

'You have to tell us all about what is happening in the Living world,' said the bald man sitting next to her.

Arjun hesitated. He did not want to reveal that he was not actually dead yet – at least not when he had left. Maybe they would jump on him and steal his life force or something. Though they certainly seemed more alive than he was at this age.

'We are here now for . . . how many years have passed?' asked the first man.

'I don't keep track in your excellent company,' said the woman.

The men cackled at this.

'You know there were these men who revolted against the British? How long ago was that?' said the bald man.

'The Mutiny?' Arjun said. 'It must be a hundred and fifty years back.'

'Yes. Start from there. What's happening on Earth?'

Arjun thought about this. So much had transpired.

'We landed on the moon,' he ventured.

They did not seem to consider this particularly wonderful news.

'What happened to the East India Company?' asked the bald man.

'I don't know. But there are giant supermarkets these days. You can walk into one and pick up anything.'

After half an hour, he was enthusiastically describing the latest Rajinikanth hit to them. The three men in the corner had left.

The old men had wistful looks on their faces.

'There is not much to do here. It's boring,' said the bald man. 'Why should the living have all the fun?'

'You have to understand, stranger,' said the first man, 'we feel no hunger or thirst. We have no urge to reproduce.'

The woman giggled at this.

'We do not know if there is meaning in death,' said the bald man.

'Can't you just leave?' Arjun asked.

'How? We have no death. We cannot kill ourselves. There is no escape,' said the woman.

'Some of these young kids,' the bald man gestured expansively with his hand. 'They think they have figured out how to get out of here. Simpletons. I think it is like that jail in Vellore, you tunnel from one cell you reach another one.'

'Are there better gurus?' asked the woman, trying to change the topic. 'Have you made some progress in that end, better philosophies in this age, at least?'

'You asked about the East India Company? There are

thousands of such corporations now. In the Living world, we are all kept busy working for them and buying from them. We do not think much about philosophy anymore.'

They sat silent for some time, depressed.

Arjun slapped his hands on his knees and said, 'But we have found the meaning of life. It is shareholder profit.'

After leaving the chief's office, Veer stood outside for some time, watching the busy lane. To the left were the living quarters for the guards. On the right, a little way off, closer to the centre of the castle, there was a crypt, and a tomb-like structure. He made his way there.

There were two men playing dice in the front room of the tomb. They looked surprised to see a visitor.

'Nobody ever comes here,' one of them said, by way of explanation.

'I need to see the Vaishala scrolls,' Veer said.

The men led the way down a cavernous set of steps, heading below the tomb. Behind a couple of locked doors were the scrolls collected at different times by the wise men, the siddhas of Panchala.

The room was musty and seemed wet.

'The water seeps in,' said one of the men.

The scrolls were in rolls, suspended from hangars in rows that extended for some distance.

Veer walked slowly among them.

'The Vaishala are at the end,' said the man.

A thousand years back, the castle of Panchala did not exist. The small community that had settled in that narrow fertile area had faced a crisis that would have eliminated Ahi, or at least their corner of it.

The siddhas who fought back against the evil of that era had then written its history and added it to the growing scrolls of the city. These were the scrolls of the era of Vaishala.

Veer walked among the scrolls, opening some, ignoring others.

Finally he stopped at one end. One of the scrolls had an illustration of a narrow weapon, shaped like a lightning bolt. He inspected it for some time.

The Vajra.

The scroll said the powerful weapon had been brought into Ahi, at the behest of a living man. It had the power to destroy or dismember a spirit of Ahi. The old men who had written the scrolls described it with awe and fear.

The wise men had decided to ban the weapon forever. The presence of the Vajra could destroy their world and their way of life as free people.

Veer turned the page.

'The powerful Vajra, weapon of Indra, forged in the waters of the Vaitharani, by the evil collaboration of Koothan of Nallore . . .' said the scroll.

A living man of Nallore had worked with a spirit of yore. A man who had stepped into Ahi while alive, a thousand years back.

In Veer's lifetime he had known only one man who had managed to do that. But Idumban had come in just a few years back.

How was the Vajra created, in this age? Was a human working with someone in Ahi again?

The thought sent a chill through him.

He climbed back up the stairs. The men were still playing dice.

'Anyone come here recently?' asked Veer.

'Nobody comes here,' said one man.

'Wait,' said the other. 'Vellaya Thevan came here, a few weeks back. There was a man with him. That man came back a couple of times after that.'

'Who was he? What did he look like?'

'Tall. Dark. I don't know his name. Vellaya Thevan seemed to treat him with respect.'

Veer left the tomb.

॰

Veer went back to his house outside the castle. He packed a few belongings and left again on his horse. He had no explanation for the domestic animals in Ahi either. They were like the spirits – they never got tired, never felt hunger, or thirst. They usually wandered around the settlements and did not seem to mind being used.

Beyond the castle, the greenery extended for a few kilometres. Several small hamlets were scattered there. The rocky desert started after this, and extended a long way. Close to Panchala a few hills dotted the desert, but after that, it was just flat and gray as far as the eye could see. Veer had crossed it a couple of times: it was a gruelling journey. He hoped he would not have to go into the desert this time. His resilience had worn thin over the past few years.

He reached the hamlet of Ponnur in a short while. The man who had been brought to him that morning, dead, was from Ponnur. As he made his way through the streets, a few women noticed him. They started following him.

He stopped the horse and said, 'Where is the house of Saamy?'

'We will take you there,' they said.

As they walked with him, the women asked him about the dead man.

'How can he just leave? Where is he?' they asked.

'He is not anywhere. He has ceased to exist,' said Veer patiently.

The women's anxiety grew. Would some of their own companions cease to exist? What was this new idea? They thought they were here to stay.

'We have to find the person who did this,' Veer said.

They seemed more shocked.

'He was killed?' asked one of them.

'Yes, I think so,' he said.

'But by whom? I did not know someone can kill another in Ahi,' said the woman.

Veer sighed. 'I do not have all the answers. We have to investigate,' he said.

They reached Saamy's house. His friends were sitting there, talking in the veranda.

Veer got down from his horse and took a look around.

The house was at a corner of the hamlet. A little way off, he could see where the desert rocks started. The greenery was getting sparse here.

He looked at the small garden in front of the man's house. It seemed unkempt. He stepped into the veranda.

'You all knew him well?' he asked.

'He was close to us, companion and guide,' said a man.

They opened the door to the house for him. Veer went in. The light was shut out here. He squinted, from habit. It did not help.

There were a couple of bookshelves and several game boards on the floor. The residents of Ahi mostly entertained themselves with games.

'He was found dead here?'

'Yes. A short time back.'

Veer scanned the floor to see if he could spot anything significant.

He walked out again and looked at the garden. It bothered him.

'Why is this not maintained?' he asked.

One of them said, 'He was keeping to himself of late. We would see him talking to himself and generally looking upset.'

'Did anyone of you speak to him recently?'

A short man stepped up. 'He was not what he used to be,' he said. 'He used to be fun, joking and happy in general. Kept a clean house and neat garden.' He hesitated and then stopped.

Veer looked at the garden carefully. Then he started pulling out the weeds. They all clustered around him at first. Then a few left and the others soon followed.

Veer worked on the weeds for some time. The short man came back.

'I have something to tell you,' he said. Veer stood up.

'Saamy was very strange the last few days,' said the man. 'He would talk to us about a place called Limbo.'

'Limbo?'

'Apparently this place, Limbo, is described in the Christian religion. They call it an abomination, against God. Created by evil.'

Veer nodded. 'And?'

'Saamy said Ahi was the Limbo mentioned by the Christians. He said we were in sin, living in a place created by evil.'

Veer looked at the garden.

'So he lost interest in living here?'

'Yes, he had been spending time with some strangers.'

'Where are they?'

'I don't know. Do you think they finished him?'

'This is the first time I am hearing about them. Strangers came here? From which hamlet?'

'I think they were from over there,' the man gestured towards the desert.

Veer shielded his eyes and stared in that direction.

'No one lives there,' he said.

∾

In the hamlets close to Ponnur, Veer found a few men who shared their concerns. They reported that a few men had been holding meetings and stirring up trouble. They had converted over to the 'cause'.

Then, just a few miles from the castle's East Gate, he had more luck. The village of Meenoor was holding a meeting in their common hall. They were deliberating on a new proposal.

He left his horse outside and walked in. The hall was full. On the stage, there was a group of men. One of them was walking back and forth.

'And what of this life as we call it?' he asked the crowd in front of him.

'We are forgotten by the world of the Living. We are at their mercy, our settlements and people destroyed by their wars and pestilences. What is our purpose? To hang on forever in this evil Limbo? We feel neither hunger, nor thirst. Roaming around as pure spirits. A challenge to God's order in every way. Let me ask you, what is the purpose of this existence?'

There was a murmuring in the room.

'If given freedom, do we dare to choose? If shown a way, do we dare to follow? If shown the passage, are we ready to pass through it? Eternal freedom. True death. That is what the leader promises you. Let us undo Satan's work,' he said.

There was a brief pause during which the gathering shuffled and whispered among themselves.

Veer stretched his legs. *'If shown the passage, are we ready to pass through it',* the man had said. It triggered a vague memory in him, something he had read a long time back. He tried to recall it, but the details escaped him.

The man on the stage smiled.

'There is only one thing that stands between you and total freedom,' he continued. 'The castle and its protectors.'

∾

Veer sat at the edge of the road going into the desert. He thought about what had transpired in the meeting.

The dead man, Saamy, could have been killed by one of his village people, but Veer did not think they had access to the Vajra.

If Saamy was killed by his new friends, the strangers who came and talked to him about Limbo, then he had to find them.

A large number of people entered Ahi from the world of the Living every day. But the space in Ahi was huge and the humans usually spread out into small communities in different areas. Panchala was one such, but he had heard of tens of thousands of such communities. One scroll mentioned that there were more people in Ahi than currently living on Earth.

But people did not travel far; they had no reason to, and

the landscape was formidable. A few enterprising men and women had gone from settlement to settlement, trying to map Ahi. They had never completed a full trip. The space was just too vast.

These strangers worried Veer, but his immediate interest was in the living human. Someone had crafted the Vajra in live spirit. His motivation could not have been good. Perhaps it was the man who had visited the scroll crypt. Finding that man was the best place to start. His collaborators in Ahi would follow.

If a human wanted to come to Panchala, he had to come through the silver cord. When Idumban came, he landed in the hills that were a few hours' ride from the castle. Idumban had not shown Veer the passage through which he had come. It would have been too dangerous to do so.

Perhaps, the unknown man had also landed close to those hills. If so, it would be a good idea to start looking for him there.

He started riding slowly along the road. Usually it was deserted, but now he saw many men and women walking towards Panchala. Young people mostly. He gave way to some of them and then started riding faster.

A few kilometres down the road, the crowd thinned out. He could see the hills a little way off. The inn was to the left of the road. He got down in front of it.

All was quiet. There was no one in either direction.

He opened the door and walked in.

There were two old men and an old woman sitting in the centre. They did not turn to look at him.

Veer approached them slowly. They were immobile, staring straight ahead. He could see that they were dead.

He scratched his head, and scanned the room. There was no one else.

There was a back door. Opening it revealed no one either.

He came back to the dead people and looked closely at them. They showed no signs of struggle. They were sitting facing each other, indicating that multiple people had attacked them at the same time, he thought.

Veer had assumed till now that he was looking for a single murderer. This looked like more people were involved.

Outside in the dust, he could make out some footprints. He looked carefully at them. Several men had been there.

The hills stood high in the desert. Should he continue to look for the human? Or concentrate on saving the people from the wielders of the Vajra?

He turned his horse in the direction of Panchala.

Arjun left the inn and continued on the road to Panchala, thinking what a depressing world this was. The sky was gray, as were the roads.

After a half hour, Arjun saw the three young men from the inn standing by the side of the road. It looked like they were waiting for him. One of them waved in his direction.

He waved back. People were friendly here, weren't they?

As he came closer, they stepped forward. Arjun suddenly felt nervous – what if they were outlaws of some sort.

'Hello stranger,' said the man who had waved. He spoke in a clipped tone. His eyes gazed at Arjun without blinking. 'Are you going to Panchala?'

'Yes,' he said.

'Can we accompany you and offer you certain counsel?'

The way he'd said it, it did not seem like Arjun had

much choice. The two men with him stared at Arjun in the same unblinking way.

They started walking together.

'We belong to the order of the Vritras,' said the man.

Arjun nodded politely.

'You may know, stranger,' said the man, 'that this land is named Ahi. Not all the dead come here. We cursed ones end up here, because of the design of the Evil One.'

'Okay,' Arjun said.

'You *are* aware of the Evil One's machinations to influence the world of the living?' said the man.

'Umm . . . not exactly.'

'The Evil One is mentioned in the Vedas, in the Avesta of Zarathushtra and in the Christian Bible. His depredations will come to an end during the apocalypse. He is the corrupter of minds; the great deceiver, acting in direct opposition to God's will.'

'I see.'

'It is he, our great sage reveals, who has created this world we call Ahi. The holy church called this place Limbo. We are now in danger of living in a world of the Evil One's design.'

Arjun mustered some courage and said: 'Who is this great sage you speak of?'

The man smiled. 'You will meet him and share his grace shortly, if you come with us. He will help you overcome your sins.'

Of which there are many, Arjun thought. He was half expecting the creepy man to whip out a receipt book and ask for contributions.

'Now,' the man said, his tone was hitting prophetic notes, 'the time has come, to destroy the Evil One's mission.

To escape from this Limbo, an abomination in God's eyes. The sage has predicted that today we will achieve total victory over the forces of evil.'

'What do you propose to do?' asked Arjun.

The man's voice dropped conspiratorially. 'We have a friend, from the world of the Living,' he said.

Arjun gaped at him.

'Yes,' the man said. 'We are close to the end of this world.'

'I came here just in time, then,' said Arjun, smiling. The three men stared at him until he stopped smiling.

'I suggest we do not treat this matter with levity,' said the creepy man.

'Uh, sure. How can I get to the castle?' Arjun asked.

'We were hoping you would accompany us, and help defeat the Evil One,' said the man.

'Can I come some other time?' Arjun said.

A change came over the men. They stopped and two of them moved to either side of him.

'It is fortunate that you met us, stranger,' said the man. He pulled out a glinting weapon, shaped like a thunderbolt.

Arjun tried to step back, but the men at his side held him.

He heard someone shout from a distance. The man looked up distracted, but then flashed the weapon and hit Arjun in the chest with it.

Arjun tried to deflect it, but failed. He felt a searing pain and then all went dark.

∿

Veer saw the four men a little way off. As he followed them, suddenly one of the men pulled up a glinting weapon. Veer recognized the Vajra.

'Hey!' he yelled, pushing his horse to go faster. The man with the Vajra looked up at him, but still managed to hit his victim before running off with his cohorts. Veer chased after them, but slowed down as he reached the prone figure on the dusty road.

He stopped his horse and got down.

It was a young man, probably in his mid-twenties. He wore strange clothes of the current time. Obviously a new arrival to Ahi.

Veer was about to get up, when he noticed that the man was moving.

The Vajra had not killed him.

Veer stared at him as he lay moaning. He slowly put his arm under the man's head and probed.

He could feel the silver cord at the back of the young man's skull.

This man was from the world of the Living.

That explained why the Vajra had not killed him. As long as his silver cord was intact, no one could kill him in Ahi.

He stood up and pulled out his water container from his bag. Sprinkling a little water on the man seemed to have an effect. His eyes opened.

'Welcome to Ahi,' Veer said.

17

THE PASSAGE

Veer sat on a rock close to the road. His horse stood nearby. Arjun was rubbing the horse's back.

'You're telling me that Idumban sent you, here, to find Vellaya Thevan?' Veer asked.

'Yes, Sir. We believe he has possessed the mind of an innocent man.'

'That is very strange. Thevan has no way to do that,' said Veer. 'Why did those men attack you?'

'I don't know. I saw them at the inn and they left before me. They wanted to recruit me into their group, I think.'

'You were at the inn? Was everything okay there?'

'Yes, Sir.'

Veer thought about this. Someone had come in after this man left and murdered the three old people at the inn.

Saamy, who had died that morning, was killed with a Vajra. The people at the inn had probably been attacked by a group. They had the weapons too.

Then Arjun had been attacked right in front of him. These attackers had a Vajra as well.

There seemed to be a lot of Vajras floating around. Too many people had access to these weapons.

'I think those men are part of a cult,' Arjun said.

Veer turned his attention to him.

'A part of what?'

'A cult. Some kind of religious nutcases. You know . . .' he said, and struggled to find an example.

'You mean a group like the Kapalikas?' asked Veer.

'Who?'

'The Kapalikas. They were people who sacrificed themselves before Kali,' said Veer.

'Correct. Yes. These people think this world is evil and want to destroy it. They said it was like the Lim something.'

'Limbo?'

'Yes. They think this is Limbo.'

'What else did they say?' asked Veer.

Arjun thought for a while and then said, 'The man said they belonged to the order of the Vritras. He said they have a plan to achieve victory over the forces of evil today.'

'Today?'

'Yes. They have a great sage who leads them. The man also said they have a living helper.'

'Yes, I'd figured that out,' said Veer.

He got up, and straightened his clothes.

'You have arrived at a time of crisis,' he said. 'I was hoping that Idumban's visit a few years back would be the last one by a living person. You guys are just trouble.'

They started walking towards Panchala. Arjun remained silent.

The edge of the green zone and the settlements showed up in a couple of hours. Veer had been quiet the whole time.

As they travelled along the greenery, Arjun could see the great spire of Panchala rising in the distance.

'Is that the castle?' he asked.

'It is the spire. Built at the centre of the castle,' said Veer.

'Very imposing.'

Veer hesitated and then said, 'It is actually an unusual structure.'

'Who built it?'

'Nobody knows. We don't have kings or leaders,' Veer said. 'Or wars for that matter.'

'Then why build a castle?'

'Good question. Usually everything in Ahi has a utility. We do not build for grandeur or to prove a point. The castle must have had some use, a long time back. But it's vanished from memory.'

They continued on.

'Are we going to meet Vellaya Thevan?' Arjun asked.

Veer shook his head. 'I don't know where he is. We're going to the Crypt of Scrolls now. There may be a bigger problem here than your mission,' said Veer.

The small settlements they passed were packed with people standing around in groups. Some of them were talking loudly and seemed agitated.

The castle loomed ahead. In front of the East Gate, there was a crowd of men. They had constructed a stage in the open space. A man was walking back and forth on the stage and delivering a speech.

A bunch of guards were at the drawbridge, gawking at the crowd. They had never seen such assemblies in Panchala. The guards had some kind of sticks as weapons in their hands. The sticks were held uncertainly, pointed at the crowd.

Veer passed them, and walked into the castle.

ॐ

The passage.

The man from this cult of the Vritras had said, *'If shown the passage, are we ready to pass through it?'*

Many years back, during Veer's initiation into the Siddha order, his gurus had instructed him on the forbidden passage.

It was a way back into human consciousness. A passage from Ahi to the mind of any living person. A means of influencing events in the world of the Living.

The passage, his guru had said, had caused misery, in the days of yore. The sages of Ahi had then sealed it, and its very existence was now forgotten. Its location was a secret, codified in the history of the Panchalas.

If the passage was discovered, his guru had said, it would be disastrous.

If Vellaya Thevan was now in the world of the Living, possessing someone's mind, it meant the ancient passage had been discovered. He could not have gone in any other way.

He walked down the steep steps of the crypt. Arjun followed him.

They reached the bottom of the stairs and stepped into the scroll room.

The man who had conducted them there seemed nervous.

'There seems to be some trouble at the gates,' he said.

Veer did not answer.

The man left.

They walked slowly along the hangars.

'Why is this place so damp?' asked Arjun.

'It is the river, rising up here.'

'What river?'

Veer checked the scrolls as he answered.

'The river Vaitharani. It runs below us.'

'Below us? An underground river?'

'Yes, it runs all through Ahi. Wherever it rises close to the surface, we have settlements.'

'Wow,' said Arjun. 'I have heard of such rivers but never seen one.'

'Stay away from it,' said Veer.

He knelt down by a hangar and started flipping through. Arjun took a look at one of the scrolls at his level. He was surprised to find he could actually read it. The script looked strange, but he could read it.

In this manner, they say Ahi was formed. And the early men who arrived in it did not know they were dead. They wandered alone in the vast dark world.

In the Island of Sumeru, the man Kapila first met a companion, Atri. On that day, they spoke and found that Ahi existed, and their existence was eternal. They vowed to make this world free of war, and power. In their image have we grown.

From these men came the settlements. In those days the Vaitharani overflowed its banks. Existence was miserable. To save themselves and the small settlements, they commanded the Vaitharani to go deeper into the ground. On the river's passage they built powerful dams, to bind the river to her hold.

Veer stood up. He had a big scroll in his hand.

'I may be able to find something in this,' he said and walked to the end of the room.

They spread the scroll on a table and peered at it.

'So it is said that this world is a representation of the minds of humans. That it links and binds all humans together,' Veer read aloud.

Arjun smiled. 'I wish they were not so obscure,' he said.

Veer continued reading the scroll.

'What are you trying to find,' Arjun asked after a few minutes.

Veer stood up and stretched.

'A few months back it seems a man came in here, to this crypt. I think he found the location of the passage back to the human mind by reading these,' he said.

∾

They made their way back up.

'What do we do now?' Arjun asked.

'If Vellaya Thevan has discovered that passage, perhaps other people know about it. One person who may know is the chief of the guards here,' said Veer.

They started walking along the main street. There was more activity than earlier. From their position, they could see the East Gate. There were a bunch of horses and men assembled there. Many more had come to the doors and windows to watch them.

Arjun turned to look towards the spire. It towered over them, glistening in the gray light. Around its base there were ramparts. Its crown could not be seen very clearly from the ground.

The chief was not in his office. They said he was at the East Gate, commanding troops.

Veer seemed alarmed by this statement.

'What are they planning to do?' he asked the guard who had given them the information.

'It seems there is a crowd at the gate, and they are looking for trouble,' said the guard.

Veer and Arjun hurried along to the gate. The castle's walls sloped down at that point, and there were steps going up. They could see the chief up on the wall. He was yelling at someone below.

Veer ran up the stairs.

In the open space beyond the castle and across the road leading to it, there was a huge crowd now. It seemed like thousands of men and women had assembled.

'The fools want to get into the castle,' said the chief, to Veer.

On the drawbridge there were around thirty men on horses. They had the stick-like weapons in their hands. The horses seemed frightened.

'They're going to learn a lesson,' said the chief.

'You should raise the drawbridge now and seal off the castle,' Veer said.

The chief glared at him.

'I am perfectly capable of managing this,' he said.

'No doubt. This is a needless confrontation. Withdraw your men and seal the castle,' said Veer again.

The chief ignored him.

'Charge,' he yelled at the soldiers.

The men started moving slowly towards the crowd. They marched close together, and had to maintain a tight hold on their horses.

'This is going to be bad,' said Veer.

The horses started galloping towards the crowd. As they did, a few men came to the front of the mass. Arjun could see the Vajra flashing in their hands.

The soldiers galloped into the crowed. A few men and women, towards whom they were charging, screamed and tried to run. The men with the weapons stepped forward and raised their Vajras.

There were flashes of light and fire; the charging soldiers

fell from their horses, hit by the weapon. Within a few moments, the charge had ended. Most of the soldiers lay dead on the ground. The four or five men left turned tail and headed straight for the greens.

Some in the crowd cheered. Others seemed shocked at the display of the powerful weapon.

The Vritras started walking towards the castle. Part of the crowd started moving with them. The guards at the drawbridge looked up to the chief for guidance.

The chief seemed paralyzed.

Veer stepped up on the rampart and raised his hand at the guards.

'Raise the drawbridge,' he shouted.

The drawbridge had never been raised in his time at Ahi. He did not know if it would actually work or fall apart.

'Raise it,' he screamed again.

The guards fell back into the castle. A few men ran to the room from which the pulley operated.

Seeing the guards fall back seemed to energize the crowd. They started running forward. The men with the Vajras walked more calmly as the crowd surged past them.

The drawbridge creaked. It lifted a few inches off the ground and teetered there. An awful groan came from the chains.

Then it began lifting again. The guards could be heard shouting as they pulled the lever. Finally the bridge came up fully and closed the East Gate.

The crowd stopped in front of the waterless deep moat. Their leaders came up to the front, and there were consultations.

Veer sighed. 'We have bought some time,' he said.

The chief was sitting on the other side of the rampart, spent.

'You have to tell us where Vellaya Thevan is. We have a disaster on our hands,' said Veer.

∾

'I assume you know the Demons' Charge,' said the chief. 'We have been tasked with defending the castle from some unknown threat, which we have done for the past hundreds of years, with no threat ever materializing. Vellaya Thevan thought the threat was actually from the human world. You remember what happened a few decades back?' he asked Veer.

'You mean the destruction of the Western settlements?'

'Yes,' said the chief.

'Many decades back,' Veer explained for Arjun's benefit, 'there was a huge war in your world. A set of wars actually, and mass killings. These events in the Living world destroy stability in Ahi. A bunch of settlements not too far from here were destroyed by the wars, for no fault of their own.'

'Correct. Think about it, the settlements could completely disappear in minutes, because Ahi exists in the human mind,' said the chief.

'Vellaya Thevan was deeply worried that the same thing could happen at any time here. He wanted to prevent it, nip it in the bud.'

'So he decided to go back into consciousness?' Veer asked.

The chief nodded slowly. 'He thought it was the duty of the Demons to protect Ahi and the settlements around Panchala. He had been telling us we should go back and eliminate threats from the humans, before they mature.'

'That is pretty radical, isn't it?' asked Veer.

The chief stayed silent.

'Your job is to sit here and take care of the castle. Not to take offensive action,' said Veer.

The chief looked a little abashed. Then he said, 'A few months back, a man came in to meet Vellaya Thevan. He said he had found out about a major threat to Ahi, an evil man who could start a war and eliminate millions in the Living world. The stranger wanted Thevan to go in and possess the evil man.'

'That must be Soman,' Arjun said.

'Who?'

'Idumban's son. He must have come in to get Vellaya Thevan to possess Sathish, on the orders of his masters.'

The chief looked confused, but said, 'This man seemed to have found a way for Thevan to go back in and do his job.'

Veer sighed.

'I talked to Thevan about this earlier. He is too rash, too prone to mistakes. It seems the man he has possessed is innocent.'

'Possible. He did not go alone, by the way,' said the chief.

'What? Who went with him?'

'Everyone in the council went with him. All ten of them have gone through a secret passage.'

Veer looked shocked.

'No one in the council is here?' he asked.

'No. I've been left alone to manage this mess.'

'You mean ten people are possessing Sathish?' asked Arjun.

'No, they must be roaming around in the Living world,

moving from mind to mind. Free spirits, ready to possess anyone they think is a threat,' said Veer.

∾

The castle was quiet after the attack. The guards watched the crowd outside. They seemed to have settled in, gathering in groups. A siege did not make sense in Ahi, since residents needed neither food nor water. Veer thought they would be attacked any time.

They were back at the crypt, poring over the scrolls.

'This passage was sealed by the ancients,' said Veer. 'Vellaya Thevan opened it, with Soman's aid, assuming that it will help Ahi. Instead, he's caused more trouble.'

'How do you mean?' said Arjun.

'The passage can be used to destroy Ahi. A sufficient number of spirits can go back through it and disrupt the collective human mind enough, and the whole of Ahi will be destroyed. Already our existence is precarious.'

'Hold on. You are saying the crowd outside wants to get into the passage.'

'Yes. That must be their goal. It is suicidal, but it will guarantee everlasting freedom from this existence.'

He went through more scrolls.

'You are positive the passage is in the castle?' asked Arjun.

'Yes. That must be why the the castle was built in the first place. To protect the passage. It also explains why they're attacking us, to get inside.'

There was a boom from outside, and the ground shook.

'Heavy weapons,' said Veer.

Arjun was staring at the scroll.

It is this stream of consciousness that sustains us, from the Vaitharani, all through Ahi, he read. *She is our mother goddess, travelling from settlement to village; village to castle, watering the fertile lands of Panchala; Haripriya and Chenchi. Pray to her and hope that she does not rise up in anger.*

'Veer,' he said.

'Yes?'

'Have you seen the river Vaitharani?'

'No, its gates are sealed in a dam beneath the spire.'

'But you know where the gates are?'

'Yes, why?'

'Can we go take a look at it?'

'I'm a little busy here,' said Veer.

'Please, believe me, it will be fruitful.'

∽

They hurried across the castle grounds. There were more booms, and the crowd's cheers could be heard inside the castle.

'This is not a great way to organize things,' said Arjun.

'What do you mean?'

'You have a world free of hunger and thirst, where people do not have any purpose. You cannot organize a community this way.'

'What does your wisdom propose we do?'

Arjun ignored the sarcasm.

'Life on earth is no different,' he said. 'You need to create a hierarchical structure. A corporation. Something in which people are rushing around creating things.'

'We do not need anything.'

'Yes, that's the genius of it. You can *make* people believe they need a lot of things. You can then create those things. You can have competition, and it excites people. Believe me, if I send a manager from Earth here, you will not have such riots, nor will anyone complain about lack of purpose, ever again.'

Veer laughed.

'You are a funny man,' he said.

The men they saw on the streets seemed scared, but Arjun could also sense that they were excited. Perhaps they did welcome the death that would follow many hundreds of years of fruitless existence.

The spire was now close. They could see that its base was broad, and that it stood on eight pillars that rose from this base. Below the pillars, they could see a trap door. Veer pushed it open. 'This should not really be open,' he said.

'There's a reason why it is,' said Arjun. A flight of steps went down, and they began going down.

'It is just the river here, Arjun, and it's not very safe to go near it,' said Veer.

Their footsteps echoed as they descended lower and lower. The steps spiralled down, and seemed to go on for some time. They must have descended a hundred feet when the floor finally levelled.

Arjun felt claustrophobic. He looked up at the faint light coming from the top. He hoped he wasn't wrong about this.

The floor was damp. As they stepped forward, he could hear a faint steady roar coming from below.

'That would be the river,' said Veer. 'You sure you want to go down there?'

'Yes.'

Veer picked up his bag, and took out a stick from it.

'Fire in Ahi,' he said.

He rubbed the stick and it began glowing with a faint light.

Below them was a steel-like door.

'This should be locked too,' said Veer.

Arjun bent down and opened it. There were more steps, rough-hewn, going straight down. It looked like a steel ladder.

The roar became louder.

'You first,' said Veer.

Arjun put his leg on the first step, tentatively. He started going down, one step at a time. The cavity on either side was very close, increasing his sense of insecurity. The roar grew steadily. Veer was climbing down above him.

After another thirty feet, his feet hit the floor. He steadied himself, held the ladder and moved to the right. Veer came down and stood next to him. He turned his light to the front.

A few yards ahead of them there was a dam-like structure. It seemed to divert the waters of the river. On either side flowed the mighty river of the underworld: Styx for the Greeks, Nun for the Egyptians, Vaitharani for the Hindus. The river was black, but it seemed to contain a glow. It was vast and flowed with an awesome smoothness.

Arjun stepped forward slowly. The waters were deep and they could not see across to the other bank. The river entered the sluices from the left and exited to their right. The vast cavern through which it flowed had a high ceiling.

They could not see the ceiling.

Veer held up his light.

They could see several small whirlpools on the river.

'Why are we here?' asked Veer.

'Because this is the passage,' said Arjun. 'This river, this water, this is the passage. This is the way to get into the human mind, because this is human consciousness itself. The scriptures are clear, that there is a common stream of consciousness, and they meant that literally. It is a stream in Ahi.'

They stared at the river.

This was the human mind, its collective self, slowly snaking its way all across Ahi.

'So, they did not actually hide the passage. They just hid its meaning,' Veer said.

'Yes. Soman must have figured it out. I'm sure some of the people in the crowd outside are also aware of it.'

'But what is in this for Soman? Why would he reveal the passage to Vellaya Thevan as well as to the mad men of the Vritras?'

'If Vellaya Thevan controls this passage, Soman cannot use it to influence and create havoc in the Living world. He wants access to this passage, that is all. If the crowd manages to get in, I'm sure he will control them somehow and win over the passage,' said Arjun.

Veer observed the water for some time.

'So, the knowledge is out. But we can still try to close this passage permanently,' he said.

'How?'

Veer started picking up some packets from his bag.

'I have some fireworks. I am not sure they are enough though,' he said.

Arjun said, 'What about my mission? I came here to get Vellaya Thevan out of Sathish's mind.'

'Surely your mission is not as important as saving Ahi itself? Millions will die if this world is destroyed. To save a village you can lose a man,' said Veer.

Arjun stared at him.

'You know, I heard someone else say this barely a day back. She was a sociopath of the highest order. How can you sacrifice a man you do not even know?'

Veer hesitated.

'Our world faces a great danger. It is my duty to protect them,' he said.

'Yes, in the right way. Sacrificing people at your altar is not the right way.'

Veer closed his eyes.

'I can bring Vellaya Thevan back,' he said.

Veer gave his bag to Arjun and prepared himself. He looked around wistfully.

'If this passage is threatened, promise me you will seal it,' he said.

'I will,' said Arjun simply.

Veer stepped up to the riverbank. He touched its waters with his feet. It was cold.

'Veer,' said Arjun.

He turned.

'If you get to Sathish Kumar, you may want to know about a man named Anderson. He was the one who planned this scheme.'

Veer smiled.

'I will let Vellaya Thevan know.'

He waved and then waded into the water, heading straight for the whirlpools.

Arjun started the climb back.

18

THE SEALING OF THE PASSAGE

The castle was in chaos. The walls shook with some kind of explosion every few moments. Arjun stepped out of the spire's tunnel and ran along the main street to the East Gate.

The scene at the ramparts was fiery. The crowd was much bigger now; they stayed off in the open space and were cheering.

A set of men were close to the castle walls. In front of the drawbridge, stood Soman.

Tall and regal, he made an imposing figure. The men crowded around him. They all had their Vajras out.

Soman had a weapon in his hand that crackled and fizzed, as if it were a live streak of lightning. He raised his arm and flashed it at the castle wall. There was a boom, and a flash. Sections of the wall tumbled to the ground.

The crowd cheered in response.

Soman must have managed to create formidable weapons with his consciousness. They were now in his control in Ahi, and nobody had anything close. The pathetic sticks the castle guards had were not going to help.

Arjun saw the chief standing a little to the left, watching his castle fall apart before his eyes.

'You have to buy time. Veer has gone to get Vellaya Thevan,' Arjun said.

'So you found the passage?' asked the chief.

'Yes,' said Arjun.

'And they want to get to the passage?'

'The crowd does. I think Soman has other ideas.'

The chief rubbed his face.

'We could talk to them,' said Arjun.

'I have another idea,' the chief said. 'Bring me the Trumpet.'

The Trumpet turned out to be a voice enhancer, a loudspeaker kind of device.

The chief held it to his mouth and said, 'Vritras, we know what you want.'

Soman turned his attention to the voice. Arjun stepped back a little.

'You cannot get it,' said the chief. 'We have sealed the passage permanently.'

Soman laughed aloud. He did not seem to need a Trumpet. His laughter fell across the walls and rolled around the castle as if it was a narrow dome. The chief cowered.

'Liar!' he said. 'He lies,' he screamed at the crowd. 'I can see that you have not sealed anything.'

Arjun wondered what Soman meant by that. What could he see, and how did he know for sure?

But the Vajra flashed and a lightning arc made its way right toward the chief. He fell back and the wall swayed as the arc hit it with a loud sound.

They retreated down to the safety of the castle.

'What do we do now?' asked the chief.

This was strange, Arjun thought, suddenly being thrust

into a leadership position. The chief was actually looking to him for direction, presumably because he had been with Veer.

How would a leader handle this, he wondered. Faced with a group, he had always seen leaders try to divide them.

Soman seemed to be a first-rate psychopath. Arjun recalled his rashness in the sorcerer's council. It was possible to provoke him into doing something stupid. His goals could not be the same as the cult and its followers.

'Give me the Trumpet,' he said.

∾

As Soman prepared to hurl the thunderbolt again, a small figure showed up on top of the East Gate.

'Vritras, show up for peace,' yelled the figure. 'You will be delivered, but we sue for peace.'

Soman looked at the man and readied his Vajra again.

'We are brothers,' said the figure.

Soman shot the thunderbolt.

The lightning emanated from his weapon and sped towards the small figure. The man did not move. The crowd gasped, as the powerful jolt hit him. The man fell down.

As the crowd cheered, something strange happened. The figure on the East Gate struggled up again.

The figure stood up, with the Trumpet in his hand.

Soman stared at the man transfixed. How did this happen? How had the Vajra not killed? Nobody could survive a blow from it.

'God's children,' screamed the figure. 'Trust us. We are brothers and we shall be redeemed together.'

Soman hesitated. The crowd was murmuring. A few men close to him moved uncertainly.

He could try another shot.

The sage, the man whom the fools worshipped as their messiah, came up to Soman. He looked worried.

'Maybe we should talk to them,' he said.

Soman lifted the thunderbolt again.

He could hear a collective growl from the crowd.

He lowered it. The figure placed the Trumpet on the ground and put his hands together in salutation.

Soman smiled. This could still turn out to his advantage. He put his weapon on the ground and saluted back.

The drawbridge went down slowly. The crowd surged forward. Soman and Koothan walked towards the castle with their men.

As Arjun walked down the stairs from the gate, the soldiers clustered around gave him way. They looked at him with a mixture of awe and admiration.

The chief ran forward to meet him.

'How did you do that? How did you survive a direct hit?' the chief asked.

Arjun shrugged.

'We have more important things to consider. Did you station your men around the spire?'

'Yes. But there are not many of them and this crowd is huge.'

'Let us hope we can manage them,' said Arjun.

The East Gate opened, and they could see the Vritras advancing.

Arjun smiled. He was looking forward to this. It was exhilarating to be deceiving and cunning.

The chief went forward to receive the men. They met at the drawbridge's edge.

'Welcome,' said the chief, looking carefully at Soman. He ignored the sage, Koothan.

'You could all come in, but the castle has no space,' he gestured at the crowd behind them. 'Can some of you come forward with us?'

The sage stepped forward. 'You have to allow my followers in.'

Soman raised his hand.

'Only a few of us will come in,' he said to the chief. The sage looked irritated, but said nothing.

The crowd kept coming forward. The sage turned to them and raised his hands.

'Stay here, while we find out the truth behind this offer.'

The crowd seemed dissatisfied. There were murmurs of protest.

Soman, the sage and a couple of men entered the castle.

'My office,' said the chief, as he walked with them.

The soldiers in the castle gawked at the sage's flowing beard and at the powerful Soman. His formidable weapon was visible in a sheath hanging on his back.

The retinue stopped at the chief's room.

They found Arjun sitting on a chair, waiting for them.

'Arjun Palani,' said Soman. 'I was expecting to meet you.'

'And I, you,' said Arjun.

Soman laughed. 'You are going to regret this meeting though,' he said.

'You know this man?' the sage asked.

'Yes. He is a low-class worker, back from where I come,' said Soman.

'How did he survive the Vajra?' asked the sage.

'Because he is alive, like me. He cannot be killed by it. Although there are other means . . .' smiled Soman.

The chief did not seem to like the turn the conversation was taking.

'Let us discuss your demands,' he said.

'There is nothing to discuss. This world has to end,' said the sage.

Soman raised his hand again. 'Let us hear what they have to offer,' he said.

The chief shifted in his seat.

'Vellaya Thevan is not here,' he said.

'Yes, we are aware of that.'

'I assume you all know where the passage is?' Arjun asked.

'Not yet,' said the sage, glancing at Soman.

'I will let you know when the time comes,' Soman said.

Arjun saw an opening. Soman controlled the knowledge of the passage.

'The passage is under the spire,' said Arjun. 'It is the river Vaitharani itself.'

Soman looked at him surprised.

The chief spread his arms. 'We cannot take a decision to open it until Thevan comes back. We do not know when he will be back.'

'He is not your king,' said the sage.

'Ah . . .' sighed the chief. 'A king may be welcome here.'

Soman smiled. 'I believe you can find one.'

The sage stood up. 'I won't stand for this kind of talk,' he said. 'This land is Satan's spawn. We have a sacred duty to destroy it.'

'Sit down,' said Soman. 'Do not give us the bullshit you spew on the sheep out there.'

The sage looked enraged. 'How dare you,' he sputtered. Then he turned to the men with him. 'Let the command go out. We know where the passage is – we will open it.'

Soman unsheathed his weapon. The men looked from him to the sage. One man turned to leave.

Soman growled and hit him with the Vajra. The man fell to the floor, dead.

The other man fled. They could hear him running down the stairs of the office.

Soman turned to the sage and said, 'You have outlived your usefulness.' The sage stepped back, frightened. The thunderbolt hit him square on the chest. He slumped in his chair.

'Now . . .' said Soman turning to the chief. 'Where were we?'

Arjun and the chief sat, shell-shocked.

At that moment, there was a great wailing sound that washed over them.

'Here come the sheep,' Arjun said.

Men could be heard running up the street. There were loud screams from afar.

Arjun stepped out of the room; the chief followed him. From the top of the steps, they could see a great mass of people streaming into the castle. The soldiers tried to stop them, but the tide of people swept them aside. Arjun and the chief watched, awed, for a few moments.

'What do we do now?' asked the chief.

'Let us first get behind your men at the spire,' said Arjun. 'We need to protect the passage.'

Soman, who had initially come up behind them, was now nowhere to be seen. The man had an uncanny knack of disappearing.

Arjun stepped back into the chief's room. The sage and his protector lay dead. He picked up the protector's Vajra. Then they ran down the steps and fled the coming tsunami.

∞

Arjun reached the protective ring around the spire just in time. The crowd had stopped at the chief's office. They were carrying the sage's body out.

The spire loomed above them. They had not given Veer enough time to do his job with Vellaya Thevan. If the passage stayed open when the masses came in, it would be the end of Ahi.

Arjun realized he had to seal the passage, and that too effectively. Normal doors and locks would surely be torn apart by the crowd.

Some people in the crowd were now turning their attention to the spire. The sight of the soldiers seemed to have enraged them.

A couple of men started advancing with their Vajras held out.

Arjun had expected chaos, but not this soon. He looked around desperately.

What could seal the passage?

His eyes were drawn to the mighty spire.

Veer had said everything in Ahi had its utility.

What was the spire for?

The eight pillars supporting the spire rose up to the base of the tower itself.

Soman seemed to know the passage was not sealed. The only structure he could have seen from outside the castle was the spire.

The spire must be the seal.

The thought flashed through Arjun's mind.

Yes, it must have been built to seal the passage below. A seal that could not be shifted. It was massive.

It struck him that Soman was still not in sight. He seemed to have abandoned the enterprise mid-way. Or he was hanging around somewhere, waiting for Arjun to make a move.

Arjun walked around the pillars slowly.

At the central pillar right next to the trap door that Veer had opened earlier, he saw the keystone.

He looked keenly at it. Gravity was artificial in Ahi. The spire would descend correctly if he was right. If not, it would destroy the castle.

He turned to look at the soldiers. They were under assault now. The cultists pushed against them. A few of the guards fell dead from the Vajras.

Arjun hesitated. How would Veer come back if the passage was sealed?

He could see the chief running around, trying to rally his men. It was a futile task.

Vajras flashed repeatedly.

Arjun raised the Vajra in his hand. He hit the keystone with it. There was a flash and a boom. It did not budge.

The first set of men had fallen and some of the crowd was not facing any resistance.

He struck again. The stone moved slightly and cracks showed up around it.

'Finally,' he thought.

He struck again and again and the stone started coming toward him. The cracks spread all over the pillar. He pulled at the stone with his hands. As he moved it, there was a rumble on the ground. Some dust fell on him from above.

The rumble came again, and one of the pillars shook and bent.

The sound now had the attention of the fighting men. They all turned to look at the spire.

Arjun pulled again and the stone came away. Two pillars on either side buckled. The spire was swaying.

Arjun ran from under the spire's base and looked up.

With technical precision, the opposing pillars fell, one by one. The central pillar started sinking into the ground. The spire swayed as it came down, inch by inch.

The multitudes watching stood silent. Their madness seemed too minor before the magnificence of the spectacle.

The spire lowered slowly at first, and then something seemed to give way in the ground and the base came crashing down. It sank into the ground, breaking whatever was in its path. People ran away on all sides as the dust rose up. The massive base went deep into the ground.

And then it stopped. The seal was complete.

A passage did not exist in the castle of Panchala anymore.

The castle was forlorn. The cultists had taken the body of their sage and left. The sealing had taken all the fight out of them. They had also realized that the killer was from their own ranks.

The chief was going around collecting the bodies of his dead men. He had not had time to speak with Arjun.

Arjun walked around the deserted streets. He had fulfilled his promise to Veer. But in that process, he had also closed the way back for him.

Perhaps Veer and Vellaya Thevan could come back through another passage: they must exist in Ahi.

Was his mission done? He had no idea.

Arjun looked up at the sky; the grey light hadn't faded. How many hours had passed since he had entered Ahi? It seemed like a lifetime.

He stood at the East Gate and hesitated.

Perhaps he should just stay here. There was nothing to go back to.

On the other hand, hunger, thirst and pain gave life some meaning.

He started towards the desert, and home.

∼

When Arjun entered the cave in the hills, there was another man in there, waiting for him.

Soman sat by the far edge of the cave, close to the abyss. His face was illuminated by the faint light from outside.

He had a Vajra in his hand.

'Hello,' he said as Arjun walked in.

Arjun looked at the weapon.

'You're a spoilsport, Arjun,' said Soman. 'You poke your nose into things that do not concern you. I have to rid you of that habit.'

'You cannot kill me with the weapon,' said Arjun.

Soman smiled. His perfect teeth glowed in the light.

'Touch the back of your head,' he said.

Arjun raised his hand and felt the back of his head. There was a small knotted cord there.

'I just have to cut it. It will be painless,' said Soman.

Then he got up.

'I have a question,' said Arjun. 'Something unresolved yet.'

'Shoot.'

'How did you get Vellaya Thevan to believe that Sathish Kumar was a menace to society? That is your most impressive accomplishment.'

Soman smiled again. 'I did not have to do much. You

must understand, Arjun, that Vellaya Thevan himself came to that conclusion. All I did was to point Thevan at Sathish's mind.

'Every one of these guys – Sathish, Aman, even Anderson – is a Hitler or a Churchill in the making, ready to massacre millions in their pursuit for power. I just had to make Sathish act excited, which I did with the help of drugs, that is all. Marking someone like you as a villain, that is a problem. Sathish was easy prey. His deepest thoughts are already wounded.'

Arjun moved forward slowly.

Soman lifted his Vajra casually. 'This is actually quite a pity,' he said.

As he pointed the Vajra, Arjun moved closer.

Soman seemed uncertain.

'What are you trying to do?' he said.

'I am taking you with me,' said Arjun and leaped at Soman. The Vajra crackled. Arjun heard a scream as he made contact with Soman, pushing both of them back into the abyss.

His final memory in Ahi was that of Soman's terror-stricken face, as they hurtled down together.

PART III

This is the way it is with mortals after death. The sinews no longer bind flesh and bone, the fierce heat of the blazing pyre consumes them, and the spirit flees from our white bones, a ghost that flutters and goes like a dream. Hasten to the light, with all speed.

– The Odyssey, Book XI

19

THE EXORCISM

When I opened my eyes, I was not in the hut.

It was dark. My whole body hurt. I tried to move. Flashes of pain shot through my neck.

Feeling crept slowly back in my limbs. I lay still, listening to the birds outside.

I had made it back. My body seemed intact, nothing was missing.

'Idumban,' I croaked after some time.

There was no one.

I turned and sat up painfully.

'Idumban, Malini,' I called again.

I was in a room, a normal apartment room. How did I get here?

The door opened. Someone switched on the light. I squeezed my eyes shut to block the glare.

'Welcome back,' said Idumban's voice.

'Where am I?' I asked without opening my eyes.

'My humble home,' he said. 'I had to move you.'

'Where is Malini?'

There was silence.

I opened my eyes.

'Where is Malini? Sathish?'

'I don't know. Anderson's men discovered the hut. I had to move you.'

I tried to stand up. My legs felt like they were being pierced with thousands of needles.

'God,' I said, swaying. 'This nightmare never ends.'

'Did you find Vellaya Thevan?'

'No,' I said. 'What time is it?'

'Six in the evening.'

'If Anderson has Sathish, he is going to be on television soon,' I said.

'Yes. It's the final day of the Trade Centre conference. The chief minister will be there. Sathish will be taken there, again.'

'Let's go, then. I want to see what happens.'

'You're tired; you should rest.'

I looked at him soberly.

'I met Soman.'

Idumban's face clouded.

'Did he cause any trouble?'

I ignored the question.

'I have to confess something.'

'What?'

I told him.

'He fell with you, into the abyss?'

'Yes.'

Idumban bowed down his head. His shoulders shook.

I let him cry.

Soman was now a part of me, my mind. I had killed a man, pretty much, for the first time in my life. I thought of his body, wherever it was, waiting for him to come back.

We were out of Idumban's home in half an hour. He removed the sidecar from his scooter and let me get on the back seat.

The ride was silent, Idumban lost in his own thoughts. I did not have the strength for conversation either.

The Trade Centre was crowded. We parked some distance from the conference hall and walked the rest of the way. There was a lot of security, metal detectors and gun-toting policemen.

We entered the hall. The media was there in full force. There were television screens on either side of the hall that projected what the official videographer was filming.

I looked for Sathish. He had not come yet.

'Tell me what happened in Ahi,' said Idumban.

I narrated the meeting with Veer; and his quest for the passage.

'So Veer is now looking for Vellaya Thevan?' asked Idumban.

'Yes. I am not sure if he has found him.'

The doors opened and Sathish walked in slowly, supported by Aman. Anderson followed, keeping some distance between them.

Sathish looked pitiful. He shuffled along and sat down on a seat far into the middle aisle.

He slumped down and covered his face with his hands.

Aman stood by him, apparently waiting for the action.

I kept away from Anderson. Raj and Malini were probably at his mercy. It made my blood boil to see him smirking.

The videographer panned the crowd and then zoomed in on Sathish. His pose seemed to attract the attention of everyone in the hall.

'Hello,' said someone in the mike. 'We see that Mr Sathish Kumar from BSD is here. Can you say a few words about the conference, sir?'

There was nervous laughter from a few people in the crowd.

So this was the final nail.

Sathish looked up at the stage, at the man posing the question. A microphone was thrust in front of him.

He coughed and then said, 'I have had horrible nightmares.'

The crowd went silent.

'But what I am going to tell you, now, is worse than those nightmares in my mind,' he said.

Idumban looked at me.

'I am going to tell you of a real plot, an evil plan to influence world oil prices. That plot is not the most fascinating thing you will hear, though.'

He licked his lips and continued. 'No, the fascination here should be for a few macabre men, men who are so drunk with power that they would destroy the entire world for a few dollars more.'

There was a shout from the back. Anderson got up from his seat and started walking down the aisle.

'Turn off the camera,' he yelled.

As he walked, a curious thing happened. He seemed to stop and sway back and forth every few steps.

'Turn it off,' he shouted again.

Then he collapsed on the floor and lay there, writhing.

The videographer hesitated. Aman stood stunned. The media, though, had sensed a scoop. A few reporters ran forward to Sathish; some of the cameras started filming Anderson's contortions.

Sathish stood up, to be heard better. He supported himself on Aman.

'For a few dollars more,' he said, louder and steadier, 'these men have planned to unleash chaos and misery, in places they would never see; among people they would not care to know.'

He paused. Anderson had help now. A couple of his men came rushing and tried to pick him up. They pushed away the surrounding cameramen. The city being Chennai, the cameramen seemed to take it as a personal insult and pushed back. There was chaos in the aisles. Everyone in the hall was standing up now, and jostling to watch the fracas.

Sathish turned to look at Anderson.

'That evil man,' he yelled into the microphone, 'got what he deserved.'

Pandemonium broke out in the conference hall.

Idumban touched my arm.

'Congratulations,' he said.

EPILOGUE

When I came in on Tuesday, a note on my desk asked me to check in with HR. My computer was locked. I walked up the two floors to the HR department. They made me wait for some time. Finally I was shown into a conference room.

The original EXM team were there. So was Sathish. Jiten Sharma, the public relations guy, was also present.

Sathish still had dark circles under his eyes. He looked tired. The previous two days had rolled up a storm across the world and he had been hounded by media from all over.

PH Capital was not available for comment. The oil-producing OPEC countries demanded a formal inquiry by the United States government. Security experts were having a field day over the details of the Blaze worm.

The worm had been released into the wild, but mysteriously self-destructed. Symantec and other firms speculated that the original programmer had put in a feature that caused the self-destruction sequence.

There was no mention of Ahi or the sorcerers' involvement in the news. Sathish had simply said he had been drugged. WTIC had declared their horror at the Blaze worm and claimed they had worked with PH Capital without being aware of the plot or the purpose of the worm. I assumed their experimental chambers would be wiped clean. Raj and Malini, who were held there before Anderson went crazy, had been turned safely out of their offices.

I thought the managers in the conference room had reason to be happy. Instead, they looked grim.

Jiten nodded at me. Aman and the rest of the team carefully avoided eye contact.

'Arjun Palani, great job. Your role in the EXM team has exceeded expectations,' said Jiten.

You bet, I thought.

'You have followed instructions clearly. Our success is largely due to that,' he continued.

I looked around the table puzzled. This sounded like a performance appraisal meeting.

'Now, you understand you are still subject to the original non-disclosure you signed with us?'

I vaguely remembered signing a document on Friday.

'Yes.'

'Okay, good. You cannot talk to the media, or anyone outside this room about the happenings of last week.'

There goes my bestselling book, I thought. Obviously, they saw me as a problem to shower their managerial skills on.

Jiten smiled in a strained fashion. 'For your contribution, we would like to offer you an onsite opportunity. It will be a great experience for you.'

I stayed silent.

'We have a new client coming up in Tanzania,' he said. 'Great country. Friendly locals.' The smile was back.

'I would rather stay in Chennai,' I said.

'Unfortunately, we need your services in Tanzania,' repeated Jiten.

I laughed aloud. Sathish started at the sound.

'Is my firing last week still valid?' I said. 'I like that offer better.'

Nobody said anything.

I opened the door and stepped out. There goes my fourth job, I thought.

My cell phone buzzed. Raj was calling me. He was back at work in the Cyber Crime division.

'They fired you yet?' he asked.

'Yes, of course.'

'Did you tell them to at least change the damn server passwords? I can have you in their payroll forever.'

I laughed.

'I'm meeting Malini for lunch. You want to come?'

'No,' I said. 'I have another appointment.'

༄

I got out of the auto-rickshaw in Pallikaranai. Idumban was waiting for me outside the old apartment building.

'You sure you want to do this?' he asked.

I nodded and slowly climbed up the stairs. I rang the bell of the apartment and Subbu's mother opened the door. His father was watching television.

'Did you meet Subbu?' she asked.

'No,' I said.

'But I know where he is.'